ARTHUR
OF
ALBION

To Brian, Wendy and Toby: for all the dreams — J. M.
In memory of my father and with gratitude to my mother
and my wife for their help and support — P. T.

Barefoot Books
2067 Massachusetts Ave
Cambridge, MA 02140

This book has been printed on 100% acid-free paper

Graphic design by Penny Lamprell, Lymington
Color separation by Bright Arts, Singapore
Printed and bound in Malaysia by Tien Wah Press

This book was typeset in Duc de Berry and Goudy Old Style
The illustrations were prepared in watercolors with brushes and
watercolor pencils on enamel paper

Hardback ISBN 978-1-84686-049-2

1 3 5 7 9 8 6 4 2

Library of Congress Cataloging-in-Publication Data
Matthews, John, 1948-
Arthur of Albion / John Matthews ; Pavel Tatarnikov.
p. cm.
Summary: Briefly recounts various legends about King Arthur and the
Knights of the Round Table, including how Arthur came to own the sword Excalibur,
magical creatures met by Arthur and his men, and the strange powers of Merlin.
ISBN 978-1-84686-049-2 (alk. paper)
1. Arthurian romances—Adaptations. [1. Arthur, King—Legends. 2. Knights and
knighthood—Folklore. 3. Folklore—England.] I. Tatarnikov, Pavel, ill. II. Title.

PZ8.1.M433Art 2007
398.2—dc22

2006038847

ARTHUR
OF ALBION

JOHN MATTHEWS

PAVEL TATARNIKOV

Barefoot Books
Celebrating Art and Story

CONTENTS

ALBION

ong ago, in the time before time, when the world was still filled with marvels, a fair green island lay beyond the Pillars of Hercules. In those days it had many names. Some called it Merlin's Isle, after the great enchanter who worked his magic upon the world in that time. Others called it the Island of the Mighty, because of the great heroes who dwelled there. But most called it Albion, after a giant who had ruled there ages before.

Albion was a land of many wonders. Dragons hid beneath the Hollow Hills by day and came out at night to light up the air with their flaming breath. The strange creature known as the Questing Beast roamed the land. It had the hide of a leopard, the haunches of a lion, the head and tail of a serpent and the feet of a hart. Only one man could capture it, and he had not yet been born.

Fairy people from the Elf Mounds and the twilight world of Undern were often seen
there, riding under the moon on mysterious errands of their own, for in those days
there was still peace between the worlds of elves and men.

The island was divided into many small kingdoms, ruled over by strong kings. Each
wanted to be known as the greatest in the land, and often they fought with each other
to see who was the mightiest. For this reason the land grew troubled, for the people
could not rest easy in their beds at night for fear that battle and war might
overtake them and destroy their lives.

But Merlin the Wise made a prophecy that said: "A king shall come who shall rule
over these lands and as far afield as Rome herself, and his name shall be Arthur."

His words were true, for the age of Arthur would soon begin.

Arthur of Albion

Arthur was the greatest king who ever lived in the island of Albion. It is said that he had fairy blood in his veins and that this made him both wise and long-lived. It is also said that he could transform himself into a raven, and that in this form he flew all over the land searching for brave knights to serve him.

Of Arthur's Lineage

Arthur's father was King Uther Pendragon and his mother was Igraine, daughter of Avalach, whose own mother was of the fairy people. Uther fought a great war over Igraine because when he first saw her she was the wife of Duke Gorlois of Cornouaille. After the duke was killed in battle, Uther married Igraine and in time she gave birth to the boy who would one day become king.

Of His Childhood Years

There were many men who wished to kill the son of King Uther and Queen Igraine, so one night Merlin, the great wizard of Albion, came to the royal hall and took away the baby. Some say that he gave the child to the elves, who brought him up in their own world and gave him many gifts, but others say that he was fostered upon a brave man named Sir Ector of the Savage Forest whose own son, Kay, grew up as Arthur's companion. When Arthur was a boy, Merlin often came to teach him the ways of magic and the laws of kingship.

Of Arthur's Reign

When Arthur became king, he asked Merlin to build him a great city that was to be called Camelot the Golden. And at the heart of the city would be a mighty hall with twenty-two windows. And in the midst of the hall would be a round table, where all the greatest knights in the land would sit together as equals.

So it was done as the young king asked, and in time the bravest and best of the knights of Albion came to King Arthur's court, and from there they went out through the land to keep the peace and help any who were in need. Thus began the great days of King Arthur, when magic was everywhere, and Albion was safe from evil men, and dragons and monsters went in fear of their lives.

Arthur married the most beautiful woman in the land, whose name was Guinevere, and together they ruled as king and queen over the glorious kingdom of Albion. In the pages of this book, you will read of the many brave deeds and exploits of Arthur's knights, and of the part played in their fates by Merlin, whose fame as a magician and prophet has never been surpassed.

Of the Sword in the Stone

Merlin knew that there were those among the lords of Albion who would not believe that Arthur was the son of Uther Pendragon and therefore the rightful king, so he arranged for a marvelous test that would prove, once and for all, who should be king. Using his magical arts, he took a block of marble and placed within it a fiery sword, so that only the hilt showed. Then he made it so that only Arthur could free this sword. And having done that, he conjured a storm of thunder and lightning, in the midst of which the marble block with the sword embedded within appeared outside the greatest church in the land. So begins the first of these tales of Arthur,

High King of Albion.

The Boy who Became King

There was once a king of Albion whose name was Uther Pendragon. He was a strong, fierce man who made many enemies among the lords of the country. When Uther's queen, Igraine, gave birth to a son, they named him Arthur.

Merlin, Uther's wise and magical counselor, who knew everything that had happened and was going to happen, came to the king and said: "Sir, there are many evil people in your kingdom who would like to do you and your family harm. It would be better to send the child away until this danger is past."

And the king, though he was sorry to do so, agreed.

So Merlin took the child in his arms and carried him away, in the depths of night, to a castle deep within the great dark forest. There, he gave the boy into the care of a brave and faithful knight named Sir Ector.

Sir Ector and his wife had only one child, who was named Kay. Arthur and Kay grew up together like brothers, neither of them knowing that Arthur was the king's son.

Years passed and King Uther grew sick. Knowing that he would soon die, he sent word to Merlin to bring his son home.

But King Uther died before his wise old friend could do as he commanded.

The land of Albion had no king.

The strongest of the lords began to quarrel amongst themselves over who should succeed the old king.

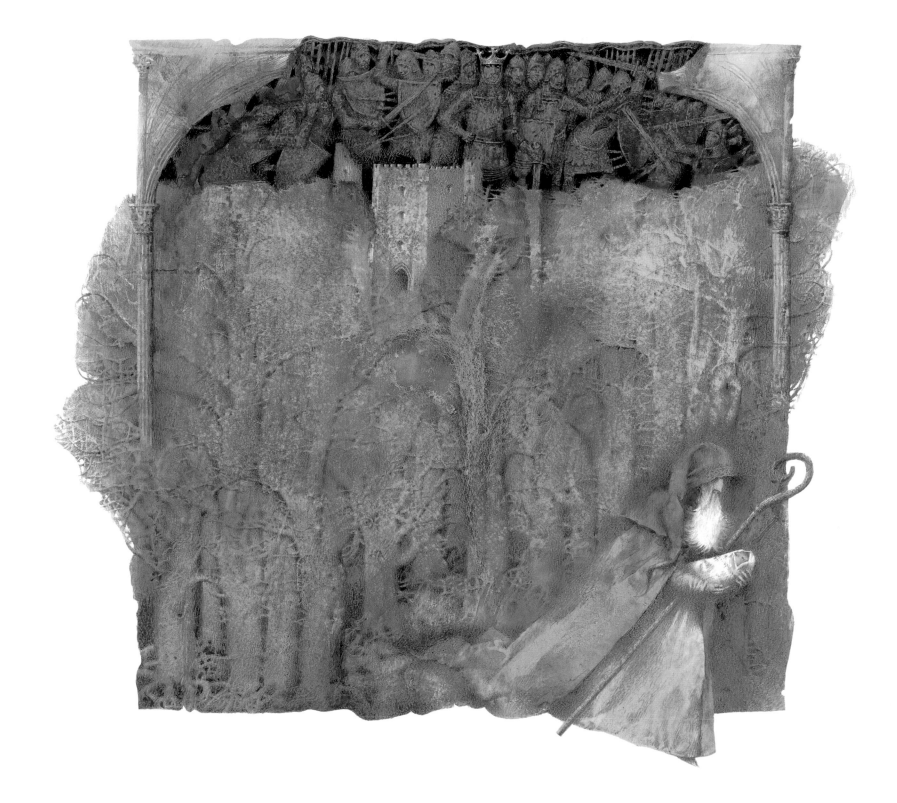

Then, one day, a strange thing happened. A big block of marble appeared outside the greatest church in the land. Stuck into the stone was a fiery sword. On the stone was written in words of gold:

WHOEVER PULLS THE SWORD
FROM THIS STONE
SHALL BE KING OF ALBION

The Archbishop came and looked at the sword in the stone and declared that there should be a contest. He said: "Let everyone who thinks he should be king come here on Christmas Day and try to remove the sword."

So it was done. People came from all over Albion. Many camped in the fields around the great church. The knights put up their bright silk tents and built large fires. The poor folk slept on the hard ground.

On Christmas morning, after everyone had been to church, a great crowd gathered around the sword in the stone. Everyone wanted to see who would pull it out and be the new king.

The knights and lords formed a long line that went three times around the church. Fights broke out over who was to go first.

All day the strongest men in the land gasped and groaned as they struggled to pull the sword out of the stone. But, try as they might, not one of them could move it so much as an inch.

At the end of the day, when no one had managed to pull the sword from the stone, everyone went back to their tents or houses.

Next day it all began again, but still no one could move the sword. The knights and lords began to get restless. Then Merlin arrived and declared that there should be a

tournament, in which everyone could show how strong he was.

The knights thought this a good idea, and everyone who was not trying to pull out the sword went away to the fields to set up the lists, where the knights could test their skills.

Now among the crowd who had come to watch the pulling of the sword were Sir Ector and his two sons, Kay and Arthur. Kay was a big, strong youth, and of course he wanted to try his hand at the tournament. But he had left his sword behind at the inn where they were staying.

"Arthur, go back and fetch my sword," Kay said. "I'll give you a penny if you do."

So Arthur, who was a kind and gentle boy, set off back to the inn.

When he got there, he found it was locked. Everyone was out, watching the tournament.

Arthur hurried back to where Kay and Sir Ector were waiting. On the way, he passed the big block of stone standing unattended outside the church.

Just for that moment Arthur forgot about the magical sword they had come to see. All he could think about was how angry Kay would be if he failed to bring him a weapon.

Without even thinking, Arthur climbed up onto the stone. He looked around and, seeing there was no one nearby, pulled the sword out of the block in one swift, easy movement and ran back to where Kay was waiting for him.

"This isn't my sword," Kay said. "Where did you find it?"

"It was in a big block of stone," replied Arthur.

Kay stared at his brother in amazement. He knew at once that this meant Arthur was to be king. He went to tell Sir Ector, and the next moment the knights and lords were

crowding around Arthur, telling him to put the sword back into the stone and take it out again. He did as they said, at which many people began to cheer.

"We have a king!" they cried.

But not everyone was cheering. Some of the more important lords began to ask who this Arthur was. Some of them said that they didn't care who he was, others that they did.

For a while it looked as though fighting would break out, but at that moment Merlin himself appeared and explained that Arthur was really Uther Pendragon's son, and the rightful ruler of Albion.

So everyone went off to the great church, where they crowned the boy king, amid much rejoicing.

But there were those among the lords of Albion who did not rejoice, for they believed that Arthur would be a puppet king, brought to rule over them by Merlin. They were concerned that it would be the magician who would be the real power in the land.

So eleven of these lords banded together and raised an army against the new king. And for a while there was war again in Albion. But the young King Arthur was triumphant and with Merlin's help overcame all his enemies and established his kingdom.

Then Merlin used his magic to build a great castle, which would be ever after known as Camelot the Golden, for it shone like the sun over the land. And within the castle he made a great hall with twenty-two windows, and within the hall he placed a round table big enough to seat a hundred and fifty people.

"Here all the bravest knights in the land will come," said Merlin. "And because it is a round table, no one will feel more important than the next man."

"What a wonderful idea," said Arthur. "I will call them my Knights of the Round Table."

And so it was done. All the best and bravest men came to sit at the Round Table, and with his magic, Merlin saw to it that every seat had the name of the knight who sat there engraved in letters of gold upon it.

King Arthur made them all promise that they would use their strength to do good, to help those weaker than themselves, and to defeat anyone who tried to do harm to others, especially to women and children.

He also made them promise that whenever they went in search of adventure, they would always tell him what had happened when they returned. "In fact," said King Arthur, "from now on I will not sit down to dinner until I have heard a tale of adventure or of some marvel!"

This became the custom at Camelot for as long as Arthur was king, and many a tale of adventure was told in that great hall.

THE LADIES OF THE LAKE

During the reign of King Arthur there lived in Albion certain women of power in whose veins ran the blood of the ancient fairy people. All possessed great magic, which some used to help the king, and others to hinder him, each according to her will. Many of the greatest challenges faced by the Knights of the Round Table came from these women, for they often sent strange knights or other, darker creatures to test the courage of Arthur's men.

OF THE NINE AND THEIR POWER

Together the Nine represented the ancient power of Albion from before the time of Arthur. They were led by Argante the White. At her side were the dark siblings Morgana and Morgause, whose hatred for Arthur was unmatched; Ragnall, who won the heart of the great knight Sir Gawain after her brother, the Summer Lord, released her from a spell that made her foul by day and fair by night; and Nimue, who some say beguiled Merlin himself, and when he refused to instruct her in the secrets of his magic, imprisoned him beneath a great rock. Then there was Cundry, the Earth Woman, who guided the Quest Knights in their search for the Grail; Ganeida, a prophetess who saw all that was to happen in times to come; and Dindrane, whose blood was used to heal and to bring visions. Lastly was Ceridwen, the Corn Woman, who guarded a cauldron of beaten bronze from which dead warriors returned to life though unable to speak of what they had seen in the lands beneath.

OF ARGANTE THE WHITE

The strongest of the Nine was Argante, who lived beneath the gray waters of a lake at the base of the mountain of Yr Wydffa. She it was who brought King Arthur the magical sword Excalibur, which was called forth from the molten heart of the earth's core and fashioned by elvish smiths. She had little love for Merlin, whose magic was different from her own, yet she often aided King Arthur, sending one or another of her maidens to warn him of acts of betrayal or the coming of dark forces into his realm.

OF MORGANA LE FAY

Morgana, the Crow, was Arthur's half sister, born of the marriage between his mother Igraine and Duke Gorlois of Cornouaille, whom Uther Pendragon slew in battle. Seeing Arthur as a usurper of her family, Morgana hated her half brother and became his implacable foe. Often she sent fair-seeming gifts to Camelot that were intended to harm the king, as when she sent a damsel with a poisoned mantle to Queen Guinevere. But Merlin saw through this plot and made the damsel put on the mantle first, at which she fell stone dead upon the ground.

Another time Morgana stole the great sword Excalibur and gave it to the dark knight Accolon of Gaul, whom she loved. But Arthur regained it and slew Accolon, making Morgana's hatred even stronger. The scabbard, which protected all who wore it from harm, Morgana kept and threw into a fathomless swamp, since when it has not been seen by men.

Now I shall tell you the story of how Arthur first came by Excalibur.

How King Arthur First Came by the Sword Excalibur

Though he was lord of all Albion, King Arthur had in him still the hot blood of youth, and whenever he could he liked nothing more than to escape from the court and go out alone into the wide world in search of adventure. Often Merlin would follow, out of concern for the safety of the king, watching where he went.

One day King Arthur slipped out of a little gate in the walls of Camelot and rode north along the secret paths of the Golden Wood. After a time he came upon a grim knight sitting in an ornately carved chair beneath a tree. The knight seemed to sleep, but he had a naked sword across his knees and his helmet and shield lay close by him on the ground.

Smiling a little, King Arthur donned his own armor, which was plain so that no one should recognize him, and crept toward the sleeping knight. When Arthur was still several paces away, the man opened his eyes and said: "If it is battle you seek, I am more than ready to give it."

Then he stood up and the king saw that he was very tall and strong and of an age that spoke of many battles.

"By what name shall I call you?" asked Arthur.

"I am Pelles of the Isles," answered the knight.

"And I am the Knight of the Savage Forest, who seeks adventure," said Arthur, using the name of his adoptive family.

"Then let us go to it," said King Pelles grimly.

Arthur drew his sword, the same that he had pulled from the stone to prove himself king, and the two advanced toward each other.

They began by circling like planets around the sun, but soon fell to beating out the ancient music of battle on each other's shield and breastplate and greaves.

At first King Arthur had the best of it; then King Pelles gained ground. For a time Arthur's youth gave him the advantage, then Pelles' battle-hardened strength began to tell.

Hard and fast they fought, until Pelles struck a particularly powerful blow and King Arthur's sword shattered into fragments.

Grimly, King Pelles came on, but at that moment Merlin, who had observed the battle from the shadows of the wood, raised a hand and spoke two words, which halted the knight in his tracks.

There stood Pelles, mouth open, eyes wide, his sword raised, but unmoving, held fast by the wizard's spell.

Arthur turned upon his mentor in anger. "This is unknightly and unchivalrous!"

"But it has saved your life — which is not yours to throw away so lightly," answered the wizard. "You forget that you are the king now, not some knight engaged in errantry."

Arthur had the grace to look downcast. He gestured toward the frozen knight.

"You have not killed him?"

"He will awaken an hour from now," said Merlin, "and he will be none the worse for his adventure — though I have no doubt he will be puzzled as to how he came to be standing in the middle of the clearing, with his sword drawn and no one to fight."

Arthur looked at his broken blade.

"I have no sword," he said.

"Fear not," answered Merlin. "I know of another. One that was prepared for you many years ago."

The king and the wizard rode on through the Golden Wood until they came to a valley where a dark, still lake of water lay, reflecting the clouds in the sky above it.

There Merlin stood a long while, staring out across the water. It seemed to Arthur that his lips moved, though he could not hear what it was the wizard said.

Then, as Arthur began to grow restless, he saw the dark waters move and break, and from them rose an arm in whose hand was clasped a great sword that flashed and gleamed in the sunlight like a fallen jewel.

"What wonder is this?" asked Arthur.

"It is your sword," said Merlin. "Its name is Excalibur, which means Cut Steel. With it you may never be defeated."

"But how may I get to it?" Arthur said, staring in amazement at the mighty weapon.

"You should take that little boat," answered Merlin, and Arthur saw a small craft drawn up by the lakeside, though he was sure it had not been there moments before.

The king found that the boat needed neither pole nor oar, but moved by itself upon the water until it came to a stop by the arm that held up the sword. Arthur looked down into the depths but could see nothing but darkness. Uncertainly, he stretched out his hand to take the sword. At once the hand in the water relinquished it and the arm withdrew beneath the water, leaving not even a ripple behind it.

King Arthur clasped the great sword to his breast as the boat carried him back to the shore. He stepped out and examined the weapon more closely. It was held by a scabbard of red leather, tooled with golden thread — a magnificent thing in itself. Such power thrummed in the hilt that the king's arm trembled until he drew the sword, which flashed like a burst of sunlight, and seemed to catch fire in his hand.

"This is a wondrous blade!" he cried aloud.

"The fires of the earth's heart are locked within it," said Merlin. "It was brought out of the deep core of the earth and fashioned by elvish smiths. There is no other weapon like it in all the world."

As the wizard spoke there came along the margin of the lake a woman, tall and bright as a spear of gold.

"Let the sword be used well," she said to

Arthur. Then just as suddenly as she had appeared, she was gone, though the king knew not to where.

Merlin spoke her name: "You have just seen Argante, whom men call the Lady of the Lake. She it was who commanded the sword to be made — in readiness for one who was to come. For you, Arthur."

More than this the wizard would not say, but as they followed the road through the depths of the wood toward Camelot, he asked: "Which do you value most, the sword or the scabbard?"

"Why, the sword," answered King Arthur at once.

"You are wrong to do so," said Merlin. "For though the sword is the greatest weapon ever forged, the scabbard is of greater value, for he who wears it cannot be wounded in battle. See that you guard it well."

Thus it was that King Arthur came by Excalibur, and as Merlin had told him, he was never defeated while he carried it. But later the scabbard was stolen by Morgana le Fay and where it is now, no man may say.

As for King Pelles, in due time he awoke from the spell Merlin had cast upon him, and not long after he came to offer his services to King Arthur. And if his new liege lord seemed somehow familiar, neither spoke of it, and in time Pelles became one of the greatest Knights of the Round Table.

Magical Creatures

In the time of King Arthur, many mysterious creatures roamed the land of Albion. In the depths of the Golden Wood lived green men made of leaves, and dwarves who knew the secret ways through the forest. Other creatures, more ancient still, dwelled beneath the hills and crags.

Of Giants

A giant cat plagued the kingdom for years until it was slain by Sir Kay, while in the mountains to the north and west, ancestral giants still lived. King Arthur himself faced one such at St. Michael's Mount in Cornouaille. The giant had terrorized the neighborhood for months, killing not only sheep and cattle but humans also, roasting all without remorse over a slow fire. Arthur fought the monster for a whole day before finally dispatching it with a blow from Excalibur.

Of Tristan's Dragon

Many knights made reputations as monster-killers. Sir Tristan the Sorrowful, one of Arthur's greatest knights, fought a dragon and received a poisoned wound that would not heal. Only the skills of Isolt of Eriu would work against this ill, but when Tristan first caught sight of her it cost him dear, for he fell in love with Isolt, though she was promised to his uncle, horse-eared King March of Cornouaille.

Of Dark Knights

Jaufre, a young knight who was among the first to join the Round Table fellowship, encountered what he thought was a powerful warrior as he journeyed by the shore of the sea. Only when he fought with his adversary did Jaufre discover that he was all of one piece. Horse, man, armor and weapons, all bled black blood when he hacked at them with his sword. When dead, the creature was found to be more fish than flesh.

Before coming to Camelot, Sir Lancelot, who had been brought up by the Lady of the Lake, visited the Perilous Chapel in search of his true lineage. There he was forced to do battle with black-clad knights whose blank helmets hid their grinning skulls and red-eyed stares. As Lancelot hewed them down, their armor fell to pieces and was found to be empty.

Of the Great Boar

Among the greatest challenges faced by the Knights of the Round Table was the hunt for the great boar Twrch Trwyth, which rampaged across the land, laying waste to everything in its path. In the tenth year of Arthur's reign, the king with all his heroes followed it across the island, until finally Arthur's hound Cavall brought it to bay and Arthur himself, with Kay and Bedwyr, sent their great spears into the boar's bristled body, speeding it to its death.

Of the Questing Beast

Of all the wondrous creatures that roamed the land, the strangest of all was the Questing Beast, whose true name was Glatisant, and whose history was as strange as its appearance. Hunted by successive knights, only one of whom was destined to capture it, it wove a mysterious pattern across the forest-hidden hills and valleys of Albion . . .

How King Arthur met the Questing Beast

ing Arthur was out hunting in the Golden Wood. The trees whispered together and he was soon lost, separated from his knights. After a time he found himself in a green meadow beside a spring.

The king dismounted from his horse to drink from the spring, then he lay down beneath a tall tree to rest. Sleep soon overcame him, but he woke suddenly when he heard the sound of dogs barking.

Thinking the hunt had overtaken him, Arthur sat up. By the spring was the strangest creature he had ever seen. It had the hide of a leopard, the haunches of a lion, the head and tail of a serpent, and the feet of a hart. Even stranger was the sound of barking dogs that came from within its body. Only when the creature drank from the spring did this cease.

The king kept very still, watching.

The creature drank its fill and then ran heavily into the trees, the sound of barking hounds once again issuing from within it. Scarcely had the creature vanished from sight when a tall knight came riding swiftly across the meadow. Catching sight of the king, he demanded his horse, for his own was spent.

"Tell me first your name, and why you ride so furiously through the wood?" demanded Arthur.

"As to my name, it is Pellinor, King of the Out Isles," replied the knight. "As to my business, I have no time to speak of it here, save to say that I am bound upon the adventure of the Questing Beast."

King Arthur agreed to let Pellinor take his horse on condition that he returned to Camelot one month hence and told the story of his quest.

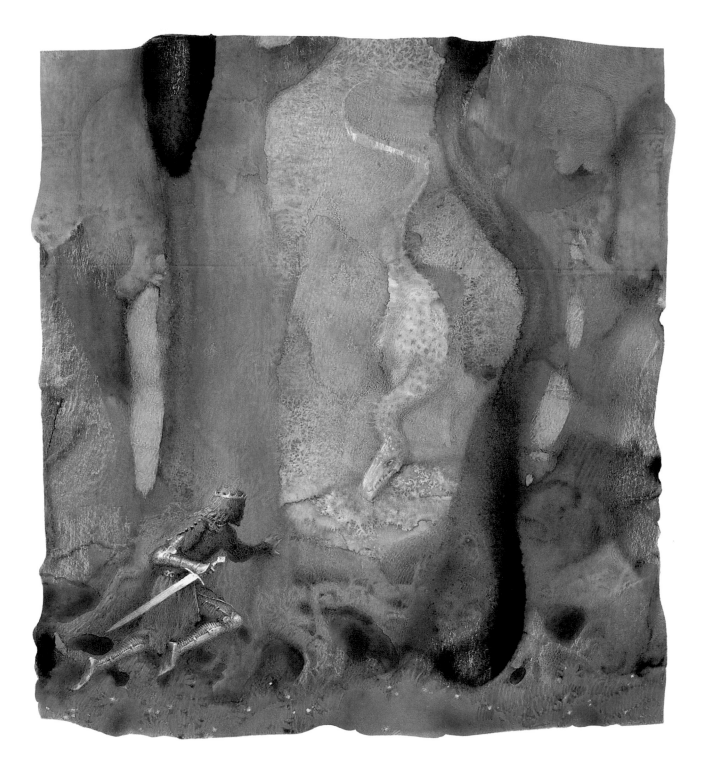

Pellinor promised and then rode off at a furious pace, following the trail of broken branches and trampled earth left by the Beast.

King Arthur sat down and dwelt on how he must seek the road back to Camelot for himself. Then there emerged through the trees a young boy, who bowed and asked if he had seen a strange beast come that way.

"What do you know of the Beast?" demanded the king.

"All and more," answered the boy.

"Foolish!" said Arthur. "How could you know of this creature — and you so young? Be off with you!"

The boy walked away and was soon lost amid the trees. Shortly after, there came an old graybeard with a wise look about him. He too came up to where the king sat and asked if he had seen the Beast.

"That I have," answered Arthur. "What can you tell me of its history?"

"As much as the boy who came this way just now," replied the old man. As he spoke, Arthur saw that it was in fact Merlin who stood before him. Then he was ashamed, for he knew that the child had been Merlin also.

"Next time, don't let an outer appearance deceive you," the wizard said sternly, though he was smiling. Then he told King Arthur all about the Beast. How its true name was Glatisant, and how it had roamed the land of Albion since time began.

"No one knows whence it comes," said Merlin. "Nor have I been able to discover any more of its history than this. Yet many men have tried to capture or kill it, and thus it is known as the Questing Beast. Only one man is fated to bring its life to an end, but that man is not yet born. In the meantime it is King Pellinor of the Out Isles who follows it — he whom you lately met."

It was to be many days before King Pellinor arrived at Camelot. When he did at last, he came with bowed head, for he had lost track of the Beast amid the tangled thickets of the Golden Wood and believed it to be far away. Then King Arthur requested that he should stay a while and join the Fellowship of the Round Table. "For we have need of strong knights," said the king, "and until such time as the Beast is rumored to be in these parts again, you may serve us if you will."

To this Pellinor gladly gave his assent, and for long years thereafter he served King Arthur faithfully. But every so often he would go in search of the Questing Beast, though always without success. It befell later that Sir Gawain and his brothers, Agravain and Gaheris, sought out Pellinor and slew him; for they blamed him for the death of their father, whom Pellinor had slain in the Battle of the Eleven Kings, soon after King Arthur was declared King of Albion.

So for a time the quest of the Beast was ended, though rumor of it still came to Camelot out of the Wildlands to the north. Then one day a young knight named Palomides came to the court. He was a great knight for all his youth, and his skin was as dark as midnight, for his father was a Saracen

and his mother of Ireland. Sir Palomides was sorrowful and rode alone, for he had fallen in love with Isolt of Eriu, who was loved in turn by Tristan the Sorrowful, one of the greatest of King Arthur's knights. But Isolt was wife to horse-eared King March of Cornouaille, and of this came great sorrow, for King March was filled with hatred for Sir Tristan and had him slain, and because of this Queen Isolt herself died of grief.

Then Palomides was likely to die also, so great was his sorrow. But now as he rode in the Golden Wood, he came to a spring and saw there a strange beast with the hide of a leopard, the haunches of a lion, the head and tail of a serpent, and the feet of a hart. From within its body came the sound of many hounds barking. As he looked in wonder, an old man appeared and told Palomides that this was the Questing Beast, and that it was his to follow.

"This adventure is for you alone. Before this it was the task of King Pellinor, but since he is dead the adventure now falls to you."

Then he vanished away, Palomides knew not where.

From that day, Palomides followed the Beast, filling with this task the empty place left within him by the death of Isolt. The days grew into years and still he followed it without success. He grew thin and wasted from his endless search, but whenever he seemed likely to catch the Beast, it fled before him. Always by day it followed the sun, and by night wandered without direction, pausing only twice each day, to drink from whatever stream or spring it could find.

Then one day, Sir Palomides' horse fell dead under him from the fury of the chase, and so he went on foot until he came to a place where a spring poured forth amid tumbled rocks.

There he found the Beast intent upon drinking, and saw that there was but one way in and out of that place. Therefore he drew his sword and rushed upon the Beast and struck it to the heart. But where it fell to the earth lay not the body of a beast, but that of a beautiful maiden and around her were a dozen white hounds that awoke and ran off into the wood barking. Then an even greater wonder occurred — the maiden woke also, and looked upon Palomides. And as he looked upon her, the old ache in his heart, that had been there since the death of Queen Isolt, went from him, and he fell upon his knees and begged the maiden to marry him.

To this she agreed, for it had long been destined that he who killed the Questing Beast should marry her. So Palomides and the maiden returned to Camelot and told King Arthur all that had befallen. And the king was glad to know that the quest was ended at last, and he caused the story to be written in a letter and placed in a box upon the tomb of King Pellinor.

As for Palomides, he married the maiden and they lived long and happily together, and Palomides became known as one of the greatest of the Knights of the Round Table.

But of the mystery of the Questing Beast there is no more to tell.

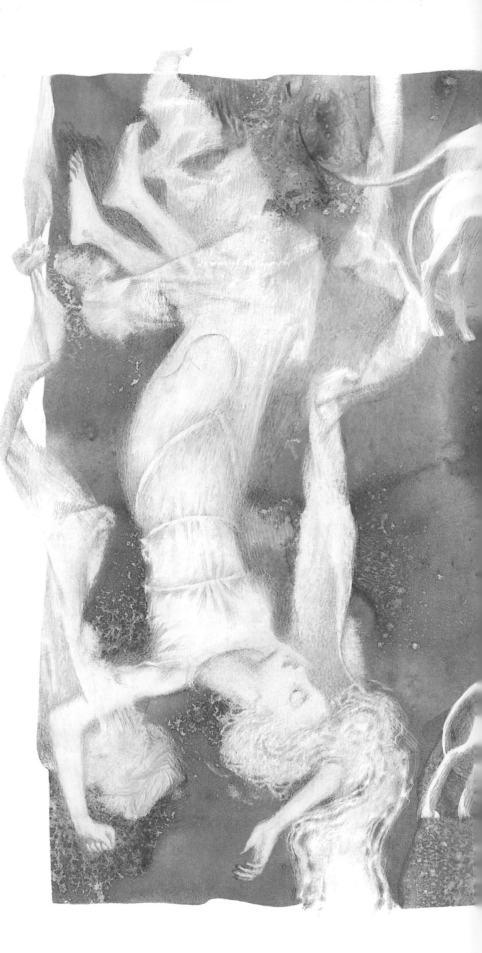

Camelot and the Round Table

When Arthur had been king for only a short time, he asked Merlin to build him a castle and a city that would serve as enduring reminders of the great vision of a unified kingdom in Albion. It took the wizard nine days and nights to bring about this feat, and taxed even his great skills. To build it he used the bones of mountains clothed with timber from the Golden Wood and marble carved from the Valley of the Blue Stones. He hung it with tapestries woven of ancient starlight and the memories of the Ages of Bronze, Silver, and Gold.

Of the Great Hall

The walls of the Great Hall were pierced by twenty-two windows, which let in the sunlight and laid patterns across the floor in which dreams could be seen. Here too Merlin placed statues of the eleven kings whom Arthur overcame before he could call himself High King of Albion. In the Great Hall he set the Round Table, made from timbers of the First Tree and decorated with patterns of constellations more ancient than those that then filled the night sky. Here the Knights of the Round Table met to share their adventures and encounters with the folk from the Otherworld, to speak of ancient mysteries, and to bring harmony to the land of Albion. Here too were held the great feasts at which so often came those who would challenge King Arthur and his men to undertake some new adventure. In this time the Great Hall was the heart of Albion, for while it remained standing, great glory came to the land.

Of the Round Table

Around the Table, Merlin set one hundred and fifty seats, each one inscribed in golden
letters with the name of the knight who would sit there — though many were not
yet born. In time all were filled by knights whose names will never be forgotten.
Here sat Lancelot the Spear Bearer, the Queen's Champion; Gawain the Lord of May;
Bedwyr the Keeper of the King's Table; Gareth Golden-hair, who could shoot
an arrow through the joint of a bird's leg; Kay the Tall, who could hear a fly stretch
its wings seven leagues away; and Culhwch the Pig Keeper, who won the golden shears
from the back of the Great Boar. These, and many more whose stories shall be told until
the book of time is closed, sat at the Round Table.

Of the City and its Treasures

Beneath the city were galleries and caverns where Merlin wrote the Books of
Broceliande and his own prophecies, and where he delved into ancient time and brought
back wonders to show the king and his court. Here, for a time, before he withdrew into
the Hollow Hills to dream away the ages until the return of the king, Merlin hid the
thirteen treasures of Albion, which included the Horn that must never be blown, the
Sword that could not be drawn, the Chessboard that played by itself, and the king's own
Scarlet Mantle of invisibility, decorated at each corner with apples of gold. He gave to
this place the name by which it is remembered still: Camelot the Golden.

After the time of Arthur, horse-eared King March of Cornouaille destroyed the
Round Table and broke down the walls of the city. Soon the ruins returned to the
elements from which they had been formed and winds blew away even the dust that
remained until there was no trace of Merlin's greatest work. But the thirteen treasures
remained hidden deep beneath the earth, and were never seen again in the lands of men.

The Quest for the White Hart

The time came when King Arthur decided to take a wife. He chose Guinevere, daughter of old King Leodegrance of the North. People called her "Guinevere the Golden" because her hair was the color of sunlight; yet her eyes were dark as smoke and full of wisdom.

The wedding took place amid great pomp and splendor in the bright month of May and was followed by a lavish feast. Yet even now the king was reluctant to eat until he had heard tell of a wonder. Merlin smiled and said: "Wait a short while and your wish will be granted."

So the whole court sat down with the king's wedding guests at the table in the Great Hall of Camelot and waited.

But not for long.

There came a crashing and commotion and into the hall raced a white hart pursued by a slender white hound. Three times around the Round Table they ran, until the hound succeeded in getting close enough to bite the hart in its hind leg. At which the hart made a great leap over the table, knocking over a big knight who sat there, then ran from the hall.

This knight, whose name was Sir Allardin of the Isles, jumped up red-faced, and as the slender white hound leapt up to follow the white hart, he snatched up the dog and put it under his arm and ran from the hall.

At that moment an imperious lady rode up and made a great outcry. She demanded that King Arthur send one of his knights to bring back the hound — which belonged to her. Even as she did so, a knight who was a stranger to the Fellowship galloped into the hall and, seizing the bridle of the lady's horse, rode off with her.

In the silence that followed, King Arthur could not help smiling a little at this strange sequence of events. But Merlin said sternly: "Do not make light of this, for it is the first quest of the Round Table. Set three of your ablest knights this task: let one bring back the White Hart, have the next bring back the Slender White Hound, and the third bring back the lady who was carried off."

Then the king called upon his nephew Sir Gawain, who was called the Hawk of May, and young Sir Tor, the Cowherd's Son, and King Pellinor, who until recently had followed the Questing Beast. Sir Gawain he commanded to bring back the hart; Sir Tor to recover the hound; King Pellinor to return with the lady.

The three set forth, each going his own way into the dark forest. Gawain took with him three hunting dogs, which soon caught the scent of the White Hart and set off in pursuit. All day long they gave chase. At last they came to a castle, where they cornered the hart in the courtyard. Gawain's hounds brought down and killed it there and then, and the knight cut off its right forefoot to prove to the king that he had achieved his quest.

Scarcely had he done so when the lord of the castle came running into the yard and railed against Gawain for killing the White Hart, which belonged to him. Then he drew his sword and killed all three of the knight's dogs.

Gawain had loved his dogs and flew at the lord of the castle in a rage. Swords clanged. Sparks flew. Gawain was the better fighter, and soon the lord hugged the earth, begging for his life. Such was Gawain's fury that he forgot his knightly vows and raised his sword for the kill.

At that moment a lady ran across the yard and flung herself protectively across the body of the fallen lord. It was too late for Gawain to stop his blow and to his horror he saw the lady's head fly from her neck. In his haste, he had killed her!

Then the fallen lord gave a cry and begged Gawain to kill him too: "For that was the lady I loved best in all the world," he said, "and now I have no reason to live."

Sadly, Gawain sheathed his sword. "Sir," he said, "I have done enough killing for one day." Then he told the man to ride to Camelot and to tell the king all that had befallen there.

Then Gawain, wearier than ever before in his life, laid down to rest. And in the morning, with a heavy heart, he made his way back to Camelot, where he first gave King Arthur the White Hart's foot and then made himself ready to be judged for his crime.

For the first time, King Arthur and Queen Guinevere came together in judgement. They decided that Gawain had acted in haste but with no ill will. Therefore they decreed that he should go unpunished, but that he should be made to swear an oath to protect all women wherever he went. To this, Gawain swore, and ever after he was known as the Knight Who Served All Women, for he never broke his oath to the king. Thus ended the first part of the quest.

Sir Tor rode as swiftly as the wind. When he was only a few miles from Camelot, there appeared in the road before him a hunch-backed dwarf who struck the knight's horse such a blow on the nose with a staff that it reared up and almost threw its rider.

"Why did you do that?" demanded Tor.

"To get your attention," growled the dwarf.

"You have it," said Sir Tor. "To what end?"

"That you will fight the red knight who waits over by that pavilion."

"I am on a quest for King Arthur," said the knight. "I will not stop for this foolishness."

"Nonetheless, you will fight him," said the dwarf, and out from a silken tent among the trees came a knight in red armor, who set his spear in rest and rode at Sir Tor full tilt.

Swift battle followed, with much giving and taking of blows. But in the end the red knight lay wounded at Sir Tor's feet.

"Go and salute King Arthur in my name," said Tor. "Say that it is the knight in search of the Slender White Hound who sent you."

The red knight promised and Sir Tor made to continue on his way, but the dwarf stood in front of him and said: "Sir, I know what it is you seek and I can take you to it. All I ask in return is that you take me into your service."

"Very well," said Sir Tor, and the two rode on together until they came to a green pasture where two bright pavilions stood like flowers in the midst of the field.

"There," said the dwarf, pointing to the tents.

Tor drew his sword and looked in the first tent. Within were three lily-white damsels fast asleep. In the second tent was a beauteous lady, also sleeping. At her feet lay the Slender White Hound. When it saw Sir Tor, it began to bark madly, waking both the lady and her three damsels.

Sir Tor seized the dog and gave it to the dwarf to hold.

"Will you take away my dog?" demanded the lady angrily.

"I will," said Tor. "For so I have been charged by my liege lord, King Arthur."

"You shall not have it for long, I promise you," vowed the lady. But Tor ignored her and rode off with the Slender White Hound tied to the dwarf's saddle.

They had not been long traveling upon the road when they heard the sound of a rider approaching and were overtaken by a big knight on a wild-eyed horse. It was Sir Allardin of the Isles.

"Give back my lady's dog, or pay the price!" bellowed Sir Allardin.

"I will not," replied Tor.

So they set their spears in rest and rode toward each other and struck each other great blows. But Sir Tor was again the victor, for even Sir Allardin was no match for him.

But as he stood over his fallen opponent a damsel ran up, calling upon Sir Tor.

"Sir," she cried, "in King Arthur's name, I beg you to grant me a request. I ask for the death of this knight. He took my brother's life and I ask for his in return."

Sir Allardin, fearful now for his life, began to beg for mercy.

"What can I do?" said Tor. "When you could have begged for quarter, you did not.

Now this damsel has demanded your death in King Arthur's name. I cannot refuse her."

The knight struggled to his feet, threw down his sword and turned to flee. Sir Tor struck without thinking, severing Sir Allardin's head from his shoulders with a single blow.

So it was that only two nights after Sir Gawain had returned to Camelot, Sir Tor rode back with the Slender White Hound and relayed all of his deeds. King Arthur praised him for bringing back the dog, but not for the death of Sir Allardin, which seemed to be without good cause.

Last of all we turn to King Pellinor, whom King Arthur had sent to bring back the lady stolen away by the stranger knight. So eager was he to achieve this task that he vowed that nothing would distract him from his course.

When King Pellinor came to a crossroads and saw a damsel sitting under a tree, cradling the dead body of a knight in her arms and weeping most sorrowfully, he gave no heed to her cries but rode on.

Soon he heard the clanging of lance on lance and came to where two knights fought hard against each other. And to one side he saw the very lady whom he had come in search of, guarded by two squires. King Pellinor rode up and said: "Madam, you must come with me to King Arthur."

"I shall do so gladly," replied the lady, whose name was Nimue. "But these knights may have something to say about it."

"The one in the red surcote is my cousin Sir Melliot, and the other is Sir Bliamor, who carried me off against my will from King Arthur's court."

King Pellinor turned his attention to the fighters and called upon them to stop. They ceased fighting at once and Bliamor ran at King Pellinor full tilt with lance at the ready.

The knights were well matched but Bliamor was tired from his combat with Sir Melliot. King Pellinor soon had the advantage and dispatched his opponent with a great blow.

At this, Sir Melliot advanced toward King Pellinor, but Nimue called out that Pellinor was from the court of King Arthur and meant her no harm.

The two men laid down their lances and, at the Lady Nimue's wish, went to a small abbey close by so that Sir Melliot's wounds could be dressed.

In the morning, they passed the crossroads where the damsel had cradled the dead knight in her arms, and there they found the bodies of both, lying together as if in sleep. The damsel had died from grief at the death of the knight. King Pellinor was saddened at this sight, for he believed now that, had he stopped, he might have saved her. He did what he could for both the dead knight and the damsel, carrying their bodies back to the abbey and paying for them to be buried next to each other and for masses to be said for their souls.

Then King Pellinor, the Lady Nimue, and Sir Melliot rode on their way until the towers of Camelot shone golden in the evening sun, and there they were greeted warmly by King Arthur and the whole court.

King Pellinor told the story of his adventure and relayed his sorrow at the death of the maiden. Then Merlin stood up and said gravely: "The damsel whom you refused to help was your own daughter, whom you had not seen since she was a child because you traveled so far and so long in search of the Questing Beast."

King Pellinor wept bitter tears at this, for it seemed to him the cruelest blow fate had ever dealt him. But Merlin took pity upon him and said: "Though this is a grievous matter, it is the way of the world that such actions are balanced by others. The knight who was slain was he whom your daughter loved best in all in the world, and she would have married him had he not fallen to the sword of the very Sir Bliamor whom you fought to save the Lady Nimue. So you see that justice has been done in the end, though these are sorrowful things."

So ended the quest for the White Hart.

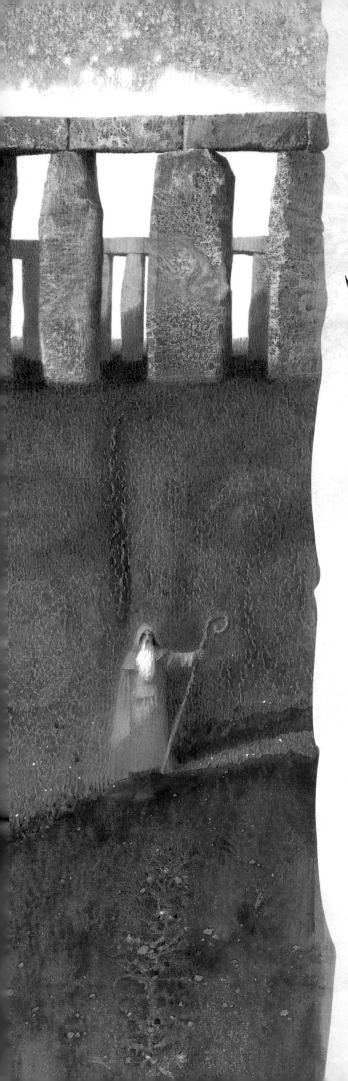

Merlin the Wise

No one knows how old Merlin is. Some say he woke in the depths of the ancient forest and that he grew wise from listening to the speech of the trees. Others say that an ancient wise man named Blaise, to whom he used to return every few years to relate all that had taken place in Albion, taught him; but that is not certain.

Of Merlin's Powers

Merlin possessed great and subtle powers. He went often to the Elf Mounds to visit the earthwise beings who lived there. From them he learned the patterns the stars make in the heavens, and the true names of plants and stones and animals, so that ever after he could call on them for help. When the young King Arthur was losing his battle against eleven kings of the northern lands who sought to destroy him and rule over Albion in his stead, Merlin made the trees of the wood called Bedegrayne come to life and march like soldiers in ranks, overwhelming the king's enemies.

Another time he brought the stones of the Giant's Dance out of the misty land of Eriu, making the stones so light they could be floated across the narrow sea to the shore of Albion, from where they were carried to the plain of Sarum and set in a circle that will stand for all time.

Of Merlin and Albion

Albion itself was once known as "Merlin's Isle," perhaps because of the mighty wall of brass that he built around it. This he made to keep out the dark things that always sought to enter the rich green lands where the moon shone in the dewponds and the birds sang songs of such beauty that the sun came out to hear them.

Of Merlin's Prophecies

Merlin was known to be many things. At first he was known as a prophet who could read the future in the stars. He predicted the coming of King Arthur himself, and foretold the day when the Holy Grail would appear at Camelot the Golden. When still a boy, he showed the tyrant Vortigern of the Thin Lips why a tower he wanted to build would not stand. Why? Because two dragons, one red and the other white, fought every day beneath the hill and shook the earth.

Of Merlin's Last Days

Merlin's own end is as uncertain as his beginning. Some say that he fell in love with a beautiful fairy woman, Nimue, one of the Nine Ladies of the Lake, and that she placed spells around him that kept him in an enchanted place forever. But others tell it differently: that he grew tired of the follies of men and returned to the Golden Wood, where he built a house of glass with seventy doors and windows. There he is still, watching the stars turn across the heavens, and waiting for King Arthur to come again.

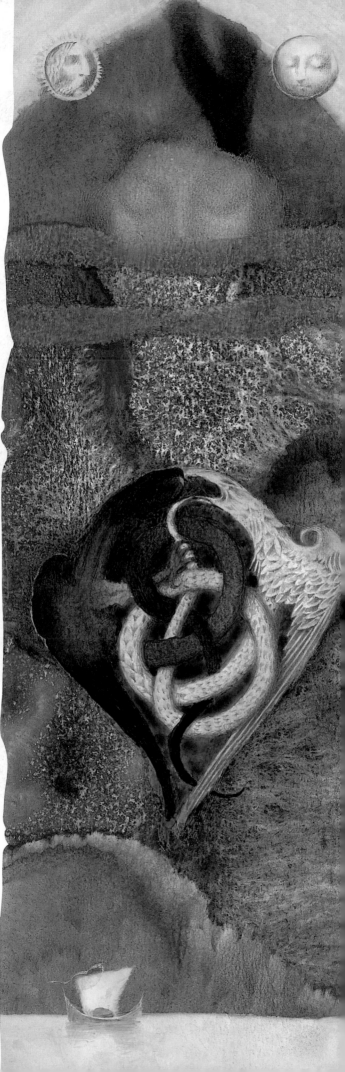

The Story of Merlin and Avenable

There came a feast day when not one of the Knights of the Round Table entered the Great Hall with a story to tell. Sir Kay looked at Sir Bedivere the Butler and both gazed anxiously around to see what they might do to ensure that the king had a wonder to listen to. Sir Bedivere's eye fell upon Merlin, who was seated, as usual, to the left of the king. "Lord Merlin," said the butler, "do you have a tale you might tell us? Surely you have seen more wonders and marvels than any one of us?"

The wizard frowned, tapping his fingers against the arm of his chair. "There is a story I could tell," he said, "though it occurred long before the days of this Fellowship and not even in this land."

"Let us hear it anyway," said Arthur, leaning forward eagerly in his seat.

"Well," began Merlin, "it happened that I was in Rome many years ago and I heard how the emperor was plagued by a strange dream. Every night he would wake up in a sweat, having dreamed the same thing again."

"What was it he dreamed?" asked Arthur.

"He saw a huge pig being chased through the city by twelve boars. Of course, being an emperor, he took this to be an omen of some kind, but he could not find anyone brave enough to tell him whether it was for good or ill.

"Naturally I knew what the dream meant, but I was not about to walk into the emperor's court to tell him. There was something else I had in mind, an injustice that needed to be set right."

"Something to do with the emperor?" asked Sir Kay.

"In a way," answered Merlin. "There was a young woman named Avenable, the daughter of a Roman consul who had been banished for an offence he had never committed. Avenable hated being away from Rome and having to live in a house half the size of the one she had grown up in, so she decided to run away and, having disguised herself as a youth, take service in the guard of no less a person than the emperor himself."

"It seemed to me that here was a way of solving two problems at once. So I devised a plan that would enable me both to explain the emperor's dream and put right the injustice to Avenable's father."

"A few weeks later, the emperor, his wife and their household — including, of course, Avenable, who was now calling herself Grisandole — were staying for a few days in a great country villa outside the city. Just as the whole family was about to dine, there came a great commotion and a huge stag with vast branching antlers and one white foot burst into the hall and stood panting before the astonished gathering. It is said, and I will vouch for it because of course I was the stag — a mere matter of the transformative will — that the beast spoke. It told the emperor that it knew of his dreams and of the one person who could explain what they really meant, and that was the Old Wise Man who lived in the forest near his palace. After which, the beast vanished."

"Of course, I was the Old Wise Man, but no one would have believed me, let alone permitted me to get near the emperor if I

had simply wandered into the palace and asked to see him. While I might have used some other method, suitably spectacular, to gain admittance, this would not have solved the problem of Grisandole."

"Well, in typically extravagant fashion, the emperor offered a huge reward to anyone who could find the Old Wise Man and bring him back for questioning. Of course everyone, including Grisandole, set off in search of the prophet; and of course they were unsuccessful. I am not someone to be found unless I want to be — which I did, in this instance, but not by just anyone."

"I waited until most of the seekers had given up — though I kept on encouraging Grisandole, showing the occasional tip of an antler or the merest glimpse of an old ragged cloak. Then I went to a clearing in the forest where I knew she was resting and, putting on the guise of the stag with one white foot again, I told her what she must do to find and capture the Old Wise Man."

"She was very obedient, young Grisandole. Taking five of her companions-in-arms with her into the forest, she set up a table with a white linen cloth over it and plenty of food. Then she lit a fire and sat down to wait with her companions."

"Sure enough, the Old Wise Man soon appeared, devoured the meal and then went to sleep, snoring like a pig in front of the fire. It was an easy task for the six of them to bind me, and then in the morning we all set off back to the emperor's palace. There I was led before him, still bound, and was commanded to explain the dream."

"The exchange that followed went thus:
Emperor: Are you the Old Wise Man?
Me: URRGGHH!!!
Emperor: I see. And do you know the meaning of the dream I have been having?
Me: Ugghh!
Emperor: He is mad. Take him away.
Me: I am most certainly not mad, sir. But I will speak only before all your nobles and your empress and everyone of the court.
Emperor (looking surprised): Very well. We shall call our vassals before us in the morning."

"And so I was taken away, bathed, fed and given a clean and comfortable bed to sleep in. Of course, an armed guard was placed outside the door, just to remind me not to think of escaping."

"Next morning we all appeared before the emperor. As soon as I saw the empress I started laughing, falling on the ground and rolling about like a madman. Which is what everyone thought I was, until I suddenly stopped, stood up and addressed the emperor in my normal voice."

"'Sir, I will explain everything to you. I laugh because of the meaning of your dream, which signifies this . . .'."

"I paused, I must admit, for effect, until I knew that I had everyone's attention."

"Then I proceeded to tell the emperor that his empress had twelve suitors who were all desperately in love with her and wanted to see her as often as they could. Being the empress, she could hardly permit this, so she devised a plan. The twelve suitors were to disguise themselves as ladies-in-waiting. That way they could see her whenever they liked and no one would be any the wiser. This was the meaning of the emperor's dream: the empress was the pig and the twelve boars that chased after her were her suitors."

"Well, what uproar then ensued. The empress and her 'ladies' were held, examined, and the truth found to be as I had described it. I then told the emperor there was another person in disguise, among his very own guard — young Grisandole."

"More uproar and outrage. But this time there was no crime intended and Grisandole had served the emperor well by finding the Old Wise Man. Apart from which, the emperor decided that Avenable — as we may call her again — was really rather beautiful, and that once he had punished the empress for her deception he would need a new wife."

"My work done, I vanished, leaving a cryptic message in letters of fire on the wall, to be interpreted later by a passing scribe, to the effect that I was both the stag and the Old Wise Man. As for the rest, Avenable's father was pardoned and his lands restored, while his daughter became the new empress."

"Which was," said Merlin, "as far as I can tell, a very satisfactory state of affairs."

Knights, their Horses, Weapons and Armor

No hero is complete without his noble steed, his mighty weapons and his bright armor. The knights took care of their armor and weapons, yet all held their horses in the highest honor, and cared for them personally with all the devotion they would show a wife or child.

Of Arthur and his Weapons

Mightiest of all was Arthur himself, whose great sword Excalibur, wrought of metal from the heart of the earth, shone bright in his hand like a flame and put terror in the hearts of his enemies. Wygar was the name of his mail shirt, and the dragon-lord's helmet was also cast in the shape of a dragon, so that men always knew when he entered the field.

But the king had other weapons: Carnwennan, his white-bladed knife that could cut the wind, so sharp was it; Rhongominiad, his spear, which could pierce armor or shield and break down walls of thickest stone; and Wynebgwrthucher, his shield, that some say had painted upon its inner side an image of the White Goddess, so that he might draw strength from her as he fought in battle against dark foes.

And whether he rode out against his enemies or on the hunt, he was mounted always upon his gray mare Llamrei, whose mane and tail were the color of smoke and who could run faster than the wind on a stormy day. And at his side went always the hound Cavall, of whom it was said that once when he rode across the part of the land known as Buelt, so great was the pace he ran that he left a footprint in the rock that could ever after be seen.

OF SIR LANCELOT

Lancelot, too, had a great horse, the color of blood, which he named Berring. And when he fought the knight Sir Tarquine, it was the horse that upheld him so that Lancelot was able to slay this evil champion of darkness. His sword was named Secace, and many warriors and knights there were in joust, tournament or battle who came to know it well, as it struck them down.

OF SIR GAWAIN

Gawain, the Hawk of May, rode always his great black steed Gringolet, and on his shield he bore the sign of the pentangle, the five-pointed star that signified his great strength and devotion to his wife Ragnall, the White Goddess of Spring. His sword was named Galatine and with it he slew many of Arthur's enemies.

OF SIR TRISTAN

Sir Tristan's mount was Bel Joeur, which he rode against the dragon of St. Sampson's Isle, and when that faithful steed was killed he took another that was named Passe-Brewel, that served him every bit as faithfully. Always his dog Husdent was at his side, as was his bow Fail-Not with which he hunted and slew many great beasts of venery.

OF SIR OWEIN

Owein said that without his horse Carnavlavc of the Cloven-Hoof, which was known as one of the Three Plundered Steeds of Albion because he stole it from the Dark King of the Dark Wood, he might never have succeeded in the Adventure of the Fountain.

OF SIR GALAHAD

Galahad it was who carried not only the Sword of the Red Hilt, which belonged to Balin the Wild before him, but also the Shield of Evelach, which had once belonged to an elf king of that name. With them he was invincible, though it was the strength of his belief that made him the greatest knight after Sir Lancelot of all the Fellowship of the Round Table.

THE ADVENTURES OF SIR LANCELOT

Of all the Knights of the Round Table, Sir Lancelot was the greatest: brave, chivalrous, King Arthur's unbeaten champion. Yet the beginning of his life was strange and fateful.

North and west from Camelot, at the foot of the mountain of Yr Wydffa, lay the gray waters of the lake — a place of great enchantment. Beneath it was a palace wrapped in mystery and strangeness, ruled over by Argante the White, eldest and most powerful of nine Otherworldly women whom many believed controlled the fate of Albion and the destiny of its kings. Here Lancelot was brought while still an infant, after the death of his parents, King Ban and Queen Ellen of Benoic, in a border quarrel. The child grew to manhood in the enchanted realm, skilled in the arts of battle and the wisdom of the Otherworld. And though he was mortal and possessed no magic of his own, he was ever after touched by the glamor of that place.

When he was fifteen, Lancelot was told by Argante that it was time to go forth into the world and seek his own destiny. "You shall be the greatest knight in all of Albion," she said. "But first you must prove yourself. Many adventures await you."

The next day, Lancelot set forth, following a wandering path that led deep into the Golden Wood. By midday the sun was high in the sky and the young man was tired. Spying a great apple tree casting its shade on the earth, he lay down to rest beneath it and fell into a deep sleep.

Soon after, there came through the forest four queens, riding on snow-white mules, with a canopy of silk held over them by their servants, misshapen men bowed down with the cruelty of the world. When they saw Lancelot sleeping beneath the tree, the queens thought he was the most beautiful young man they had ever seen, and at once they began to argue over which one of them he would come to love most.

It happened that one of the four was Morgana the Crow, King Arthur's half sister, who was skilled in magic. "Cease your prattling, my sisters," she said. "I will lay a spell upon this youth so that he shall not wake for six hours. Then let us take him with us and imprison him until he decides which of us he will love."

To this they all agreed, and so it was done. When Lancelot awoke, he was no longer lying in the shade of the apple tree but chained in a cold, dark place beneath the earth.

There the four queens came, glimmering with pale witchlight, demanding to know which of them he loved the most.

"You are all most fair," said Lancelot carefully. "I cannot possibly decide."

"Then you shall remain here until you do," said the queens, and left him alone.

Later that same day, as he lay miserably in the darkness, there came a soft voice that whispered to him from the shadows.

"How goes it with you, sir?"

"Not well," said Lancelot. "Who is it who asks?"

"My name is Laudine," said the owner of the voice. "I am a servant here. But it may be that I can help you — in return for a favor."

"I will do whatever you ask, as long as it is honorable," answered Lancelot, striving to see the owner of the voice through the darkness — but there was no one there.

The next day, the four queens visited him again, and again demanded which one of them he favored the most. Once more Lancelot refused to make any choice and once more was left alone.

In a little while the soft voice spoke again.

"How is it with you today, sir?"

"Not well," said Lancelot.

A slender white hand appeared from the shadows and set a dish of food at his side.

"Can you truly help me?" Lancelot asked.

"Tomorrow the moon will be full and the queens will be busy with their dark magic. The doors of this prison will open for a brief time at midnight. I will find a way to unlock your chains."

"How can I repay you?"

"My father, King Bagdemagus, is an old man," answered the voice of Laudine. "Next week he must fight in a tournament against an evil knight who seeks to steal our lands. If you will be his champion, I shall be well repaid."

"You have my word," said Lancelot.

Next day, as Laudine had promised, the queens did not appear. As before, the maiden brought food for the prisoner, and this time Lancelot thought he could see a dim shape in the shadows.

"Be ready, sir," said the soft voice, and before he could reply she was gone.

Time passed slowly in the darkness, then without warning there was a sound of locks clicking and doors creaking open, and a ray of moonlight pierced the darkness. As it touched the chains that bound him, Lancelot felt them fall away, setting him free.

As quickly as he could, he stumbled out of that dark and miserable place into the moonlit world. Looking back, he saw only a round dark hill where he believed there must be a castle in which he had been kept.

Before him he saw his own horse, and by its side stood a slender figure. The moonlight revealed a maiden with dark eyes and hair of white spun gold. She smiled at Lancelot and he helped her to sit before him. They rode away from the mound as quickly as they could, and as the moon set they reached King Bagdemagus' castle.

The old king was overjoyed to see his daughter and when he learned that Lancelot would stand as his champion against the evil knight who sought to seize his lands, tears shone in his eyes.

A week later, Lancelot rode in the lists against the evil knight, whose name was Sir Tarquine of the Dolorous Gard. Lancelot wore armor and bore weapons given to him by the grateful King Bagdemagus, and carried the maiden Laudine's scarf in his sleeve. In the first match, Lancelot unhorsed his opponent and the two then fought long and hard upon the ground, until Lancelot dispatched Sir Tarquine with a blow that cleft both helmet and head.

King Bagdemagus and his daughter gave him great thanks and promised they would ever be his to command. And Laudine looked with great love at the brave champion and spoke to him quietly, telling him that he should go to the castle of Sir Tarquine, which was now his by right of conquest. "For I believe you will find something there that will be of greatest importance to you," she said.

So Lancelot made his way to the Dolorous Gard, a mighty castle perched on a

crag above the sea. He was welcomed as the conqueror of Sir Tarquine, whose harsh rule had made him both feared and hated by all. There Lancelot made a wondrous discovery: For in the burial ground beside the castle he found a grave that bore the names of his own parents, and so learned that the castle was his own rightful home and that in killing Sir Tarquine he had killed the man who had slain his family.

Thus Lancelot came home at last. He renamed the castle Joyous Gard and made it a haven for all who were in need of succor. Soon after, word went out across the land of Albion of a new king named Arthur and of the great Fellowship of the Round Table where the finest knights in all the land were to sit. Lancelot answered the calling and he was knighted at Camelot on Midsummer's Day by King Arthur himself. Bagdemagus was there with Laudine, who made no secret of the love she felt toward Sir Lancelot. But he had eyes only for Arthur's queen, Guinevere, and within a year became her champion.

From that moment onward, Lancelot loved no other lady save Guinevere, and the secret burned darkly within his breast for long years after until it brought an end to the Fellowship. In that time Lancelot had become the greatest of all the Knights of the Round Table and the greatest knight in all of Albion, just as the Lady of the Lake had foretold.

As for Laudine, who had rescued him from the four queens, she never ceased to love Sir Lancelot, and in time fell sick with longing for him and ceased to eat or drink. So she wasted away and died, and with her last breath commanded that her body be placed in a black barge, which floated downriver past the walls of Camelot.

All the court came out to look upon the body of the maiden and they found a letter in her hands that told of her love for Sir Lancelot. When he saw this, the great knight wept for sorrow and had a marble tomb made for her beside the walls of Camelot.

Ladies of the Court

So many fair ladies dwelled at one time or another at King Arthur's court, it would take a year to list them all. Some are no more than names now, such as Queen Guinevere's sister Gwenvach, said to be so like her that few men could tell them apart save for the crown-shaped birthmark on the queen's shoulder.

Of Isolt

Better known is the glorious Isolt of Eriu, said to be as beautiful (or more so) than Guinevere herself, and skilled in medicine. The great knight Tristan of Leoness loved her, though she was promised to his uncle King March of Cornouaille. Because of this, their love came to nothing and both died strange deaths.

Of Lady Ragnall

Lady Ragnall, wife of Sir Gawain, came in strange manner to the court, bespelled into the shape of a hideous hag who could only be set free when her husband allowed her to choose whether she would be fair by night or by day.

Of the Fairy Woman

Sir Launfal, another of the Round Table knights, fell in love with a fairy woman who forbade him to speak of her to anyone. But in the end he was unable to resist boasting of her beauty and so lost her forever.

Of Enid

Enid, wife to Sir Geraint, was said to be the loveliest of the women of the court, save only Guinevere. Geraint won her in the Contest of the Sparrow Hawk and married her. Later, overhearing a chance remark made by Enid that seemed to cast a shadow upon his valor, he took her with him on his adventures in order to prove his strength. She proved an able companion and saved him more than once from robbers and enchanters.

Of Dindrane

When all of the Knights of the Round Table set forth in search of the Holy Grail, one woman accompanied them: Dindrane, the sister of Sir Percivale.

For most of her life she had lived as a hermit in the heart of the Golden Wood, and there she had a vision of the Grail. So many of the Quest Knights fell or were lost in darkness that soon only a handful remained. Dindrane rode with them still, and though she died upon the Quest, giving her blood to heal a sick lady, her body was placed in the magical Ship of Solomon and was said to have reached the City of the Grail before any of the knights did. There she was buried alongside Sir Galahad, who many said was the holiest knight ever to live in Albion, and who died when he looked into the heart of the sacred cup.

Of Cundry

Another who served the Grail was the dark earth maiden Cundry, one of the nine Otherworldly women who lived beneath the Lake of Avalon. She was said to be so hideous that none could look upon her without shuddering. Her task was to follow the Quest Knights and to challenge and question them at every step of the way to see that their hearts did not fail them when the going was hard, or the road difficult, or when dangers beset them on every side. Cundry's fate is not known, for when the Quest for the Grail was at last achieved, she vanished into the Golden Wood and was seen no more.

Sir Gawain and the Green Knight

One Christmas, King Arthur held court at Camelot while wolves howled in the depths of the Golden Wood and snow drifted deep against the walls of the city. At the feast, Queen Guinevere and her ladies shone in bright silks and the Knights of the Round Table were resplendent in cloth of gold.

But scarcely had the Yule Log begun to burn and the rich fare of the season been set before the company, when there came a gust of icy wind that threw back the doors of the hall and issued in a giant of a man with a sprig of sacred holly in his helm and an axe sharp enough to cut the wind in his strong right hand.

But it was not this that held everyone frozen in their place. For not only was the giant clothed in green, but also the axe that he carried and his skin were of that color, as was his long and tangled hair. But his eyes shone red.

"Who is master here?" demanded the stranger, in a voice like stones grating against each other.

"I am king," said Arthur.

"And I am the Green Knight," said the huge man. "I bring word of winter, and I offer a challenge to anyone brave enough to try it."

"I offer myself," said Gawain hotly, jumping up.

"You have not heard what I propose," rumbled the Green Knight.

"Nevertheless," said Gawain.

"Then I offer you my axe," said the Green Knight. "We shall each strike a blow with it against each other. And may the best man be the winner."

He gave the great weapon to Gawain, who hefted it and felt its weight. Then the Green Knight knelt down and bared his neck.

"Strike when you are ready," he said.

High rose the axe in Gawain's sure hands; then it fell, shearing through flesh and bone, and severing the Green Knight's head.

But as Gawain leaned on the haft, breathing hard, an outcry began in the hall. For the Green Knight did not fall. His headless trunk stood firm, and he bent to retrieve the fallen head. As he lifted it aloft, the red eyes flashed and the lips moved.

"One year from now let us meet again, Sir Gawain. Come to the Green Chapel to receive your blow. Follow the road to the north. Ask for me in winter."

With that, the Green Knight turned and strode from the hall, leaving a spreading silence in his wake and grim looks on the faces of everyone there.

Never did a year pass as swiftly as the one that followed. Spring and summer seemed scarcely born before the winds of autumn had stripped the trees of the Golden Wood and it was time for Gawain to set out in search of the Green Chapel.

Long he rode, following the way north as the Green Knight had told him. Snow and ice hung on the bare boughs of the trees and Gawain shivered each night, sleeping in his armor and with drawn sword under the cold stare of the stars.

Everywhere he asked for news of the Green Chapel and of the Green Knight, but all shook their heads in doubt.

Then one day, only three nights before the feast of Christmas, as the midwinter bonfires blazed on every hill in Albion, Gawain came

over a hill and saw a castle lying below him in a sheltered valley. He made his way there and asked for shelter.

The lord of the castle came striding out to meet him. Tall and bush-bearded, he radiated hospitality. "Welcome! Welcome!" he cried. "Welcome to my house and my home. I am Bercilak and I see by your shield that you are Sir Gawain of Orkney, nephew to King Arthur himself, and thus doubly welcome!"

Bercilak led the way inside, where servants helped Gawain disarm and dressed him in warm dry garments. Then he was led to the hall, where his host rose to meet him from beside a roaring fire.

"Here is my wife," said Sir Bercilak, "and here, her mother." Gawain bowed low to both, noting how the bright beauty of Lady Bercilak contrasted with the ugliness of her mother, whose black eyes flashed coldly upon him where her daughter's shone warm and mild.

"I seek the Green Chapel," said Gawain, as he had asked of everyone along the way.

The lord of the castle laughed: "We know it well. It is only three leagues from here. Rest you here for a while, and when you are ready we shall gladly show you the way."

A feast no less rich and splendid than might have graced the table at Camelot was set before them, and for a while Gawain forgot the shadow of the Green Knight's axe, which had hung over him all year long.

"May you sleep sound tonight," his host said as they made their way to bed. "In the morning I shall go hunting early, to catch what I can for the table. You need not attend, Sir Gawain. Rest as long as you wish. But let us agree to share anything we may win through skill or cunning on this day."

And if Gawain thought this strange, he said nothing, but bowed and crept willingly beneath the warm coverlet of his bed.

The next morning, Gawain lay in bed and listened to the noise of Sir Bercilak and his men setting forth. Soon there came a soft knock at his door, and Lady Bercilak herself entered. Smiling, she seated herself beside Gawain's bed, and engaged him in pleasant conversation. And since Gawain's skill lay not only in the wielding of a sword but also in the play of words, the lady was soon as charmed by him as he was by her.

Time passed easily until at last Lady Bercilak rose and, taking a ring from her finger, offered it to Sir Gawain.

"Let it be a token of our friendship," she whispered.

Soon Bercilak himself returned, bringing a great bristled boar he had slain and calling cheerfully upon Gawain to deliver what winnings he had from the day.

All Gawain could offer was the same bright ring he had but lately received.

"I'll not take that!" laughed Sir Bercilak. "For I'm sure it came from some fair lady. But let us consider the exchange made."

That night, Sir Bercilak proposed an exchange once more, for on the morrow he would ride out again to the hunt. Gawain he encouraged to rest: "As is right and fit for a knight of Arthur's court who has ridden hard and long in the cold lands."

And again, as the pale dawn shone out across the snowy fields, and Sir Bercilak and his men clattered over the drawbridge in search of sport, Gawain, warm beneath his coverlet, heard a gentle knock and saw the lady enter and sit by his side.

Again they spoke of this and that, and at the end of the morning Lady Bercilak kissed Gawain lightly upon the cheek by way of thanks for his company.

When Sir Bercilak returned that afternoon, proudly bearing a great stag slung across his saddle, his first words were for Gawain, demanding his spoils.

Smiling, Gawain embraced his host and kissed him on the cheek — with which Bercilak seemed well content. Yet that night, as they sat at dinner, it seemed to Gawain that Lady Bercilak's mother looked ever more harshly upon him.

"Rest you here another night," said Bercilak, "and Christmas morning you shall be shown the way to the Green Chapel." Then once again he offered to exchange whatever he should win on his third day of hunting.

Gawain woke to the noise of dogs and hunting horns. The warmth of his bed only reminded him more keenly of the ordeal that lay ahead. For surely as the Green Knight had risen living from the blow of the axe, Gawain knew he could do no such thing. He welcomed the arrival of Lady Bercilak that morning, for what better way to pass his last day than in easy conversation with so beautiful a lady?

But on this occasion Lady Bercilak herself seemed grave. "Sir," she said, "your purpose is known to me. Tomorrow you must face the Green Knight."

"You speak the truth," said Gawain sadly.

"This need not be a reason for fear," said Lady Bercilak. "I have a cure for your fate, if you will but accept it."

Then she drew forth a length of green ribbon and offered it to Gawain. "Wear this next to your skin and you may suffer no harm from any blow of the green axe."

Gawain took the ribbon and felt the enchantment within it. "I fear that I betray my knightly honor," he said. "Yet life is sweet and I am loath to give it up."

Then the lady gave him a kiss upon each cheek, and when Sir Bercilak returned, demanding his winnings and throwing down three freshly killed deer upon the floor, Gawain gave only these kisses by way of exchange, but hid the green ribbon beneath his shirt.

In the morning, the sound of silvery church bells rang out for mass. After the service Gawain asked to be shown the way to the Green Chapel. Sir Bercilak commanded a servant to accompany him and bade him Godspeed.

As the midwinter sun rose high in the sky, the road dipped down between cruel rocks to a dark valley where the light seemed reluctant to shine. Winter seemed deeper here, and the servant pointed silently into the valley and left as quickly as he might. Gawain rode on slowly until he heard a sound he recognized — an axe being sharpened. The sound came from within the mouth of a dark cave.

There the Green Knight stood, seeming taller than before, his red eyes flashing against his green skin.

"I have come, as I promised," said Gawain.

"Let us waste no time," grunted the Knight.

Gawain knelt down in the snow and bared his neck, while in his heart he thought of the green ribbon he wore beneath his shirt.

The Green Knight hefted his axe and swung it back and forth to test its strength. Then he lifted it up high and brought it down . . . to stop only a hair's breadth from Gawain's neck.

Despite himself, Gawain flinched.

"Are all King Arthur's knights so fearful?" growled the Green Knight.

"Strike," answered Gawain. "I shall not flinch again."

Again the axe was lifted and again it descended, but still the Green Knight stayed his hand at the last moment.

"Enough!" cried Gawain. "Strike and have done with it."

A third time the axe sliced air. This time it nicked the side of Gawain's neck, drawing blood that glistened on the snow.

With a cry, Gawain leapt up, drawing his sword. To his astonishment, the Green Knight stood there laughing, leaning on his axe. As Gawain looked, he saw that the Green Knight was none other than Sir Bercilak, the man who had been his host of the past three days.

"Put down your sword," Bercilak said. "This was but a test — one you almost passed. If you had not taken the green ribbon my wife offered to you, I should have spared you even this much bloodshed."

Gawain bowed his head, a red tide coloring his cheeks.

"I confess to loving life too much," he said. "But I had no magic on my side."

"Nor I, in truth," said Bercilak. "The magic was Morgana le Fay's. You saw her disguised as an old woman — my wife's mother. All an illusion — as was my appearance as the Green Knight. This I did because of a debt I owed her. It is canceled now, thanks to you."

With this, Gawain had to be content, though he judged himself harshly for having taken the ribbon. Returning to Camelot, he told all that had occurred, making no secret of his failure.

King Arthur heard him out, but declared that he should not be punished. "You are still the best of my knights, nephew," the king declared. "For your bravery I proclaim that all the Fellowship shall wear a sprig of holly about them this winter long. Let it serve as a reminder of the courage of Sir Gawain, who dared answer the Green Knight's challenge for the honor of Albion."

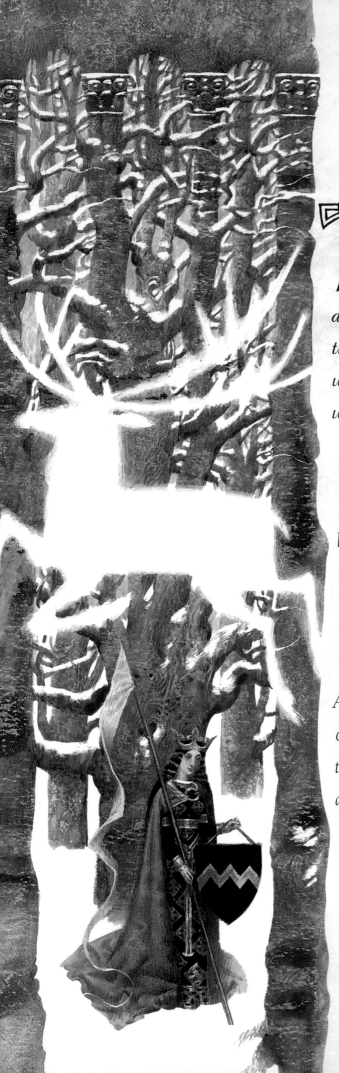

Magical Encounters

Throughout Albion in the time of King Arthur, ancient and magical beings walked the land. At certain times, especially the old magical days of midsummer and midwinter, they sought to challenge the Fellowship of the Round Table. Whenever King Arthur's court met, whenever the knights sat together at the Round Table, wonders followed.

Of the White Hart

Their very first quest began when a white hart ran through the hall at Camelot, leading three of the knights into strange adventures. Again and again, magical fairy women came to draw the heroes into the heart of the Golden Wood, there to face adversaries with terrible strengths and powers.

Of the Three Ladies

Another time, Sir Gawain, Sir Marhaus of Ireland, and Sir Owein set out in search of adventure, and met with three ladies: one ancient, one in the flower of womanhood, the third scarcely more than a child. Each of the knights chose a lady to ride with him and they set off in different directions. All faced fearsome adversaries whose strength came not from bone and sinew but from the elements themselves, bringing the endurance of earth, the rage of fire, the trickiness of water, and the strength of air as weapons to test the courage of the knights.

Of a Giant Knight

Once, King Arthur himself encountered a magical being — a giant knight named Gromer Somer Jour, whose name means "Man of the Summer Day." Against Gromer, Arthur was powerless; not even his great sword or magical shield could avail him. Gromer offered to spare the king if he could discover the answer to a dark riddle within one year. But at the year's end, the riddle was unanswered and, as Arthur rode to his promised meeting with Gromer, he fully expected to meet his death . . .

Of the Lady Ragnall

. . . On the road, Arthur met a hideous damsel, who offered to tell him the answer to Gromer's riddle — if she could marry Sir Gawain. Upon Arthur's return to Camelot, the noble-hearted knight agreed to this and King Arthur was spared. Then, on his wedding day, Gawain discovered that his bride was Ragnall, the Summer Queen. When released from the spell that bound her, she was seen to be one of the most beautiful women of King Arthur's court.

Of the Nine Maidens

Many of these encounters were said to have come about through the magic of the Nine Sisters who dwelled on the hidden island of Avalon, who by this means sent forth challenges to King Arthur and the Knights of the Round Table — to test them in their loyalty to the land and their desire to measure their strength against that of their adversaries.

The Knight of the Fountain

King Arthur held court at Carlisle and, as was his custom, asked for a story to be told before supper was served.

A knight named Sir Colgrevance described how he had come to a magical fountain in the depth of the forest. "The spring is guarded by a Black Knight, and by many savage beasts, controlled by the monstrous Churl," said Colgrevance, shuddering. "Though I survived the test of the beasts," he added sadly, "I was soundly beaten by the Black Knight."

King Arthur expressed a desire to see the Marvelous Fountain for himself. "Let the whole court proceed there at the time of the next full moon," he told his companions.

Now, among the knights present at this feast was Sir Owein, son of King Uriens of Gore. He was as yet untried, having only lately come to court. Wishing greatly to prove himself, he resolved to attempt the adventure of the magical fountain.

That night Owein secretly left the city by a side gate and, following the way described by Sir Colgrevance, soon found himself deep within the Golden Wood. He came to a clearing with a low mound on which grew a single tall, black pine tree. Under this tree was the most hideous creature he had ever seen. Man-shaped, it had but one foot and one eye in the center of its forehead. Tusks grew from its jaws, and in its mighty arms it held a club the size of a small tree. But this was not all.

Surrounding the fearsome Churl were dozens of savage beasts. Owein saw a lion, a bear, a bull and many wolves, while around these thronged many lesser creatures: stoats, weasels, ermine and wild dogs.

Though he felt more afraid than ever in his life, Owein drew his sword and advanced upon the one-eyed Churl. He did his best to ignore the animals, who, though they turned toward him and bared their teeth and growled and snarled, strangely did not attack.

The one-eyed Churl looked down upon him and said, in a voice that made the earth shake: "Why have you come, little man?"

"I have come to dare the adventure of the Marvelous Fountain," replied Owein. "Will you allow me to pass?"

"Pass?" asked the Churl. "Yes. You may pass." And he reached out with his great club and struck the trunk of the pine tree. At once all the beasts fell back, allowing Owein to pass unscathed. Soon he came to where a stream of water bubbled out of a dark hillside. There, chained to a strange green stone, was a shallow golden dish. Owein took the dish and, filling it with water, emptied it over the green stone.

Instantly the sky grew dark and thunder rolled over the forest. Lightning struck the pool, which began to boil and bubble. Then, as suddenly as it had begun, the storm passed, and in the silence Owein heard the sound of a horse approaching. There came in sight the largest knight he had ever seen, clad in night-black armor and carrying a great sword and a shield with a lightning bolt inscribed upon it.

Without speaking a word, the Black Knight saluted Sir Owein, laid his lance in rest, and charged. There followed a terrible struggle, which lasted for most of the day; but in the end Sir Owein was victorious, and delivered such a blow upon the Black Knight's helm that it shattered and gave him a wound that would surely cause his death.

With his last strength, the Black Knight mounted again on his grim steed and rode away as hastily as he could through the forest.

Though wounded himself, Owein followed the Black Knight and soon came to a castle hidden deep among the trees. The knight, bent low over his saddle, passed within.

Dismounting and tethering his horse, Owein crept beneath the entrance to the castle. Then he heard the clang of a portcullis falling in place behind him, while a second fell before him. He was trapped between the two gates and knew that soon the people of the castle would come seeking vengeance for the certain death of their master.

Then he heard a small voice say: "Sir knight, let me help you."

He saw a little window in the wall and a maiden looking out at him. "I will help you," she said again, and let fall something that sparkled on the ground. Owein saw that it was a ring.

"While you wear it, you will be invisible to all," said the maiden. "Once the gate is opened, follow me and I will hide you."

At that moment there was a great outcry from within the castle and Owein knew that the Black Knight must be dead. He put on the ring, hoping that the maiden was not playing a trick upon him. But when the gate opened and several knights rode furiously out of the castle — doubtless in search of the slayer of their master — they failed to see Owein.

As soon as the way was clear, Owein entered the inner courtyard where the maiden waited. He followed her and she led him into the castle itself and thence to a small room, where she bade him stay. "No one comes into this room but I," she said.

In the room, Owein found a small window, little more than a slit in the wall, which looked inward into the heart of the castle. Through it he found that he could see all that passed within.

He saw the body of the Black Knight laid out on a bier, with candles placed at either corner. And then he saw a dark-haired woman whom he guessed to be the mistress of the castle, weeping for the loss of her lord and cursing the one who had slain him. Soon the knights returned, declaring that they had found Owein's horse, but no sign of him.

"Continue the search," said the lady of the castle. "My lord's killer must be found. He must become the Guardian of the Fountain according to our law."

For three weeks Owein stayed in the little room, cared for by the maiden, whose name he learned was Luned.

Slowly Owein's strength returned. Each day he watched the comings and goings in the castle, and learned of its strange customs. "For as long as living memory it has been thus," said Luned. "The lady of the castle takes a husband from among the bravest knights in the land and he becomes the Guardian of the Fountain. Without this, the castle cannot survive, for the spring will cease to flow and the powers of storm and lightning will be unleashed. Thus, whoever is lord of the castle is Guardian of the Fountain, and whoever overcomes him takes his place. Many times has this happened, but you have broken this law and I am fearful of what may happen."

Owein thought deeply about this and saw how daily the Black Knight's lady grew thin and pale. Slowly the pity he felt in his heart began to turn to love.

"Soon the life of the castle will be at an end," said Luned one day. "If a new guardian is not found, we shall all perish."

"It seems to me," answered Owein, "that it is my destiny to be the new guardian."

"Yes," said the maiden, "but I fear my mistress will not look kindly upon you."

"Not if she knows it was I who slew her lord," said Owein. "But what if I were one of King Arthur's knights, come in search of the Marvelous Fountain?" For this was, after all, no less than the truth.

"Prepare yourself, for tomorrow I shall bring you to my lady," said Luned.

Next morning she gave Owein the ring that made him invisible, and he was able to leave the castle. Outside, Luned brought him a horse and his own weapons and armor, which she had polished until they shone.

Thus accoutred, and with his hair and beard trimmed, Sir Owein rode up to the gate of the castle and announced that he had come to offer himself as the new guardian.

If anyone questioned how he knew of the custom of the Marvelous Fountain, they soon forgot it in their joy at having the means to save themselves. Owein came before the lady of the castle and was made welcome. Luned stood beside her mistress and spoke of the "great deeds" of Sir Owein that were spoken of "throughout all Albion." In her eagerness to preserve her own life and those of her people, the lady agreed that Owein should be the new guardian, though of his becoming her husband, no mention was made.

So it was that Owein put on the black armor once worn by the man he had killed, and was given a steed the color of night. Every day he rode out to wait beside the spring for challengers.

Several knights came and he defeated them all. But soon the moon rose high in the sky and there came the sound of many horses on the road. King Arthur himself, with many of the Knights of the Round Table, came in search of the Marvelous Fountain, just as the king had promised he would do. Owein rode forth to meet them, clad in his black armor, so that none recognized him.

First of all, Sir Kay challenged him and was soon unhorsed. Then, in quick succession, Owein defeated Sir Bliamor, Sir Gallehodin and Sir Grummor Grummerson. Only when Sir Colgrevance advanced did he lay aside his weapons and remove his helm so that all might see who he was.

Then was there great rejoicing among the knights to see Sir Owein still living, and King Arthur demanded to know everything that had happened. So they returned to the castle and Owein revealed to the lady that it was he who had slain her lord, and confessed his love for her. If truth were told, she had herself begun to fall in love with the handsome knight, so that she felt no anger at the subterfuge but instead smiled upon him.

Before King Arthur and the court left again for Camelot, they attended the wedding of Sir Owein and the lady of the castle. Thus the ancient law of that place was upheld, and the spring continued to flow. And there are those who say that Owein defended it for long years after, while others tell that he returned to take up a place at the Round Table — but of the great Churl and the beasts who served him, no more is known.

The Grail

Of all the adventures undertaken by the Fellowship of the Round Table, none was like the Quest for the Grail. Many stories are told of this marvelous relic and rumors of the Grail's coming had been heard in Albion long before the days of King Arthur. For all this, it remained hidden, a mystery that only those fated to do so might discover.

Of Arawn and the Cauldron

Some speak of the Cauldron, an ancient vessel filled with starlight and rimmed with pearls, guarded by Arawn, the dark master of the Otherworldly realm of Annwn. Those who tell this tale say also that Arthur himself, with seven great warriors, went in search of the magical vessel, sailing beyond the edge of the world in his ship Prydwen. On the wild waters of the northernmost sea they came to a place where seven towers rose out of the deep, each one guarded by terrible warriors who spoke no words but fought like ten men.

At last, in the seventh tower, Arawn himself awaited them, his antlered head outlined against the moon. Some say that King Arthur struck a bargain with him, that in return for the Cauldron he would send his own first-born son to serve in the dark realm of Annwn.

Of the Radiant Cup

Most forgot the story of the Cauldron, if they ever knew it, until the day when all the Fellowship of the Round Table was gathered for the feast of Pentecost. Then there came a mighty wind that shook the doors and shutters of the Great Hall, and the sky grew dark. A single beam of light shone into the gloom, and within it was a radiant cup that hung there for a moment before vanishing away.

Sir Gawain, ever hasty, was the first to leap up, declaring that he would not rest until he had discovered the meaning of this wonder. One by one, all the rest of the Fellowship swore to seek the radiant vessel. And as they prepared to depart, rumors spread that this was no less a relic than the Cup used by King Jesus himself at the Last Supper. But others said that it was the ancient Cauldron returned in this new form, to test the Fellowship and to lead them into the heart of the Golden Wood.

Of the Quest of the Knights

For the first time since they had met at the Round Table, the entire Fellowship departed and left the halls of Camelot hollow and empty. As for King Arthur, he knew only sorrow, for he said: "It seems to me that I shall not see many of these great knights again." This proved true, for many fell on the great Quest and few returned to the Round Table. To this day, there are those who speak of the Quest for the Grail, while others talk of the Cauldron, but none are certain of the truth, for this quest was the greatest mystery of all that befell the land of Albion.

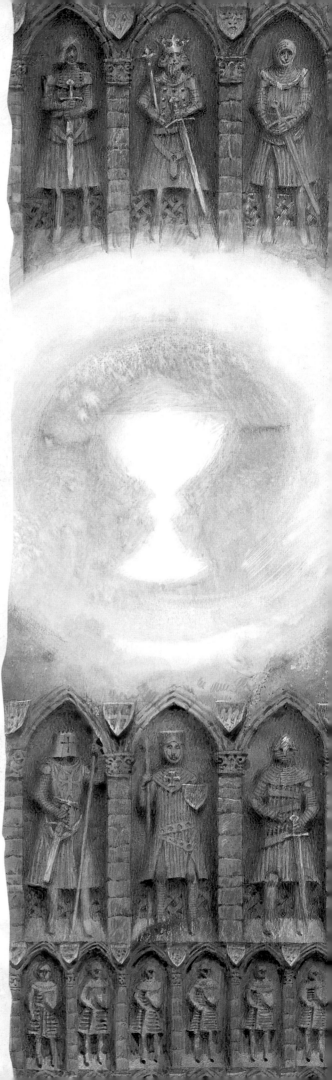

PERCIVALE AND THE QUEST FOR THE GRAIL

n the days of Uther Pendragon, King Arthur's father, one of the greatest knights of Albion was named Evrawc. But when he fell in battle against a neighboring lord, his wife withdrew from the world into the forest, taking with her an infant son whom she named Percivale.

Determined that her child should know nothing of the arts of war and chivalry, Percivale's mother brought him up in seclusion, attended only by women. But though forbidden the skills of sword and lance, as he grew to manhood, Percivale made his own weapons, fashioning a rough bow and arrows and a set of throwing spears. He became so adept with these that those who dwelled in the forest house never went without some piece of game that young Percivale brought home.

One day Percivale was in the forest when he saw coming toward him through the trees several mounted men. Dazzling in their silver skins of mail, they brought light to the dark forest. Having never seen a man in all his life, and no one dressed in armor, Percivale took them for angels and fell on his knees by the side of the track.

It happened that one of the knights was none other than Sir Gawain, and when he saw the young man kneeling there he stopped and asked if there were any wrongs to right in the name of King Arthur.

Filled with awe at being thus addressed, Percivale could only stare at them. Finally he managed to speak. "What are you?" he asked.

Looking down from his great horse, Sir Gawain said: "We are knights. Have you never seen our like before?"

"Never," replied Percivale. Then he asked: "What are 'knights'?"

The bright figure on the horse laughed aloud at that. "Go to King Arthur's city of Camelot," Gawain answered. "It lies west of here. Ask for me when you arrive. I am Sir Gawain of Orkney." Then the knights were gone, vanishing amid the trees as suddenly as they had appeared.

From that moment, all Percivale could think of was becoming a knight. Nothing his mother could say had any effect on him. Next day he set forth, riding an ancient horse and carrying his roughly made spears. Following the directions given him by Sir Gawain, he made his way through the wood until he came in sight of the walls of King Arthur's city.

Wherever he looked there were nothing but wonders: the thronging people, the mighty battle horses, the fluttering banners, and above all the knights, who rode into and out of the gates on errands of adventure.

It happened that Percivale arrived on the eve of the feast of Pentecost, when the Fellowship of the Round Table met to tell of their deeds and report how things stood in the kingdom of Albion. According to King Arthur's wish, everyone who wanted to could attend this feast, and the boards groaned with succulent boar and swan stuffed with partridge, stuffed in turn with quail.

Percivale sat amid the lesser folk and stared round-eyed at the great knights and their delicate ladies, at the king himself, who was splendid in gold and blue, and at the bard Taliesin, who sang and played as sweetly as a nightingale.

Then, at the height of the feast, came a great commotion. Into the hall rode a knight in red armor who caracoled his horse through the crowds until he stood before the dais where sat King Arthur and his queen.

Expecting some wonder or challenge, all in the hall fell silent. Insolently the man leaned down from the back of his tall horse and snatched up the golden goblet from which Guinevere herself had but lately sipped.

With a cry, the Red Knight flung the lees of the wine in the queen's face and, before anyone could move to stop him, rode forth from the hall, his harsh laughter echoing behind him.

Several of the knights leapt up at once, demanding the task of following the intruder and returning the queen's cup. Percivale stood up amid the poor folk, and cried as loudly as he could: "Sir — King Arthur — I beg you for this task, for I long to be a knight and thus may I prove myself worthy."

The king looked kindly upon the rough-clad youth, and Sir Gawain, who recognized him from their encounter in the wood, leaned close and whispered in his uncle's ear.

"So be it," said Arthur. "Let the young boy undertake this task. See that he is given a horse and weapons."

And though some of the knights murmured against this, all was done as King Arthur commanded — though in truth Percivale scarcely knew how to put on the armor or hold the great sword he was given. When he left Camelot later that day, he still carried his own rough spears and rode the great horse he had chosen for himself from the royal stable like a sack of meal.

Long and hard Percivale rode in pursuit of the Red Knight, calling out to everyone he met for news of him. But he received no word of his quarry, save for vague rumors of such a man riding north.

For two days and nights, Percivale slowly journeyed through the cold harsh lands of the northern kingdom of Gwales. When his horse was too tired to carry him, he slept beneath the stars, then rode on again at first light. On the third day, he came to a wild river and saw a man with a thin and haggard face fishing from a small wicker coracle.

When asked if he had seen the Red Knight, the man shook his head. Percivale followed the bank of the river until he saw a half-ruined castle amid the trees. Suddenly desiring the company of his fellow men, he rode up to the gates of the castle and begged to be admitted.

Kind hands helped him dismount and took off the armor he had worn without respite since leaving Camelot, and he was invited to dine at the castle. Yet they were a silent folk, very different from the company at Camelot.

There Percivale saw again the fisherman from the river — who had strangely managed to reach there before him and turned out to be the lord of the castle himself. Percivale saw that he was lame and was carried in a litter to the table, where he ate nothing.

Though he seemed distant, perhaps enduring great pain, the old lord spoke kindly to the youth, and shyly, Percivale began to speak of his longing to become a Knight of the Round Table.

As they spoke thus, a small silver bell chimed and there came into the hall a strange procession. First appeared a youth little older than Percivale himself, carrying a long spear with a white shaft. In wonder, Percivale saw that drops of blood flowed from the spearhead, falling to the floor.

Behind the youth came a fair maiden carrying a cup covered by a white cloth. Such radiance came from within this vessel that the torches that illumined the hall seemed dim by comparison.

Right up to the old lord the maiden came and offered him the Cup, from which he drank only a sip, seeming much strengthened by it. Then both the youth and the maiden departed as they had come, bearing with them the Spear and the Cup.

Percivale watched in wonder, but shyness forbade him from asking the meaning of these things. And it seemed to him that the old lord looked sadly at him thereafter. Soon he excused himself and was carried from the hall.

The next morning, Percivale found his horse groomed and saddled, his armor polished and his sword sharpened, but of the old lord there was no sign. As he set forth once again in search of the Red Knight, it seemed to him that a cloud of sorrow hung about the castle, which felt even more desolate in the light of day.

Now began a time of great trial for Percivale. Many adventures he had and more than one savage knight he defeated and sent back to Camelot to beg justice of King Arthur. Often he was mocked for his clumsy ways and many times he heard himself dubbed uncouth, foolish and simple.

Months passed and new leaves unfurled upon the trees. At last Percivale received word of the Red Knight and one day, in a part of the Golden Wood that seemed somehow familiar, he caught up with his quarry, who proudly carried the queen's goblet, suspended by a silken cord from his saddle.

A great struggle followed, in which Percivale was several times almost overcome, for the Red Knight was a mighty warrior. But in the end Percivale slew him and took back the queen's goblet.

As he turned toward Camelot, Percivale realized that he was close by the half-ruined castle where he had witnessed the procession of the Spear and the Cup. The desire to understand the meaning of the mystery overcame him and he turned aside from his path to knock once more at the castle gate.

As before, he was made welcome by the silent people of the castle, and again he saw the old lord carried in on his litter. The kingly fisherman smiled and welcomed him, but ate nothing and spoke but little, until at last the youth with the Spear and the maiden with the Cup entered. Again, the old lord sipped from the Cup and seemed refreshed. But this time, before the procession could depart, Percivale raised his voice and asked: "What is the meaning of these things?"

At once the old lord sat straighter in his chair. "Long have we waited for one who would ask that question," he said. "Many years have passed since I received a wound that has never healed. For so it was decreed that I must remain between life and death until one came with a good heart who would heal me. The Spear that bleeds is the weapon that caused me hurt — only this can heal me. The Cup alone keeps me alive."

Then it seemed to Percivale that he knew what must be done — though no one had told him. Reverently he took the white Spear in his hands, and laid the tip gently upon the old lord's wound. At once the blood that still welled from the spear ceased to flow and the old lord leapt up, crying out that he was healed at last.

Amid great rejoicing, Percivale took his leave of the old lord and made his way back to Camelot. And as he rode through the wood, he saw that on every side the trees and bushes were laden with blossoms, as though the land itself expressed its joy at the healing of the kingly fisherman.

At Camelot, Percivale was royally received, and both King Arthur and Queen Guinevere rewarded him for his great deeds, and he was made a Knight of the Round Table, as he most wished to be.

In the years that followed, Percivale became one of the greatest knights of the Fellowship. Then came the day when a vision of the radiant Cup shone out in the hall of Camelot and all the knights vowed to seek it, including Percivale.

Many said that the Cup was the Holy Grail, and a great quest began that lasted long years and claimed the lives of many of the Fellowship. In the end, it was said that only three of the knights were successful in their search, and found their way to the shining city of the Grail, where they were permitted to know its wondrous powers.

One of those three knights was Percivale, and it is further said that in the end he became the guardian of the sacred vessel, keeping it safely hidden until such time as others would come in search of it — long after the days of King Arthur and the Knights of the Round Table.

The Magic of Albion

During King Arthur's reign it was said that magic was everywhere in Albion. Behind every tree in the Golden Wood, over every hill and every valley, it lay like a mist over the land. This was an ancient magic, from before the time of kings and queens, stronger than the sinews of knights or the sharpest of swords; an old magic of bone and blood, of earth and stone and starlight.

Of the Fairy People

Much of this magic came from the fairy people, the Tall and Shining Ones who had once walked free in the land but now hid beneath the Hollow Hills and in remote mountain valleys. In Arthur's time it was said that many of these ancient beings came forth again to walk openly under the stars, and that the king's reign was marked by magic because of this.

Of the Four Treasures

Four mighty treasures the fairy people gave to mankind, which held great power and goodness within them. First was the Cauldron, which had the power to bring dead warriors back to life — though they were unable to speak or tell of what they had

seen in the Otherworld. Then there was the great Spear that cried out before battle and returned to the hand that had flung it. The third was the magical Chessboard that played by itself, the pieces shuttling across the checkered wood, changing the destiny of Camelot's bravest knights and most beautiful ladies. Last of all was the Sword that could cut the wind itself, and once it had been drawn could not be sheathed until it had tasted blood.

Of Merlin's Secret

In the first days of his reign, King Arthur himself held the four great treasures, but as the days darkened and the ending of his rule drew near, Merlin hid them and nine other treasures,   so that only the one destined to wield them, who was yet unborn, could find them. Men called these hidden things the Hallows and from their hiding place they continued to radiate magic across all of Albion.

Of Arthur's Passing

After the passing of King Arthur, these ancient treasures were forgotten, and the people of the world no longer remembered the great virtue that lay within them. But some did not forget, and among the wise there are those who still believe that a great leader will come to claim them again and to restore the old magic of Albion.

The Departing of King Arthur for Avalon

 or long years, King Arthur ruled wisely and well over the land of Albion. But in the days after the quest for the Holy Grail, in which many of the great Fellowship of the Round Table perished, a dark time came upon Camelot the Golden. The King's nephew, Mordred, the youngest son of King Lot of Orkney and the witch-queen Morgause, began to stir up dissension among the knights, whispering of the friendship between Sir Lancelot and Queen Guinevere and how they had betrayed the king. Even Arthur himself felt doubt, and was at last persuaded to have Queen Guinevere arrested and tried.

Harsh judges declared her guilty of treason and, according to the laws of the time, she was sentenced to burn at the stake.

Now, in truth, Sir Lancelot had loved the queen from the first moment he saw her; but this loyalty to the king and to the Fellowship was such that he had done no more than look upon her from afar.

Therefore, when word reached him of the queen's trial, he made haste to Camelot so that he might defend her. Arriving on the day she was destined to die, too late to speak out in her defence, he fought against her guards and carried her to the safety of his castle of Joyous Gard. But in the midst of the fighting he slew both Sir Gareth and Sir Agravain, brothers to Sir Gawain and nephews to King Arthur himself.

Thus it came about that there was war between the king and his greatest knights, and between Sir Lancelot and Sir Gawain, who had been friends but now were fierce enemies.

Dark indeed were the days that followed. While King Arthur and Sir Gawain laid siege to Sir Lancelot, Mordred declared himself king and raised an army against his uncle. Recognizing Mordred's evil plan, King Arthur made peace with Sir Lancelot and welcomed Queen Guinevere back to his side. But by now the split in the heart of the kingdom was too wide to heal, and on a fateful day a great battle was fought at a place called Camlan.

The forces of the King and Mordred's army were drawn up against each other, grim and despairing. King Arthur was determined still that battle should not be joined, and sought for terms of peace. But when a little snake slipped through the grass and bit one of that knights on the heel, the knight drew his sword to kill the creature and a flash of his blade became a signal for battle to begin.

All that day they fought, and many brave men fell upon each side. The last of the great fellowship of knights died fighting alongside the king, and in the end only a handful of men were left alive. Lancelot, who might have turned the tide of battle, remained in exile, and so came too late to save his lord.

In the midst of the field, King Arthur came face to face with Mordred, and the two men fought until the king gave his nephew a terrible wound. But with his last strength, Mordred struck King Arthur on the head so that he fell to the earth and lay for a long while unmoving. There Sir Bedivere and Sir Owein, themselves gravely wounded, found him beside the body of Mordred and carried him to the side of a small, still lake to bathe his wounds.

After a while the king stirred. Softly he commanded Sir Bedivere to take the sword Excalibur and throw it back into the waters of the lake — for he had seen that this was the same place where he had come with Merlin, long years before, to receive the sword from the Lady Argante.

At first Sir Bedivere was reluctant to throw away the sword, for its magic was part of the king's strength and thus the strength of Albion itself. But in the end his devotion to King Arthur overcame his doubts, and he threw the sword out across the water. There, amid the ripples on the surface of the lake, the sword slipped back into its old home, and afterward Sir Bedivere swore that a white arm emerged from the dark depths and caught the sword as it fell and took it beneath the waters of the lake.

Then Bedivere returned to the king and he and Sir Owein knelt by his side, fearful that he would die.

Then all at once with a sound like the chiming of bells there came across the water a small boat. Within it were three bright-faced ladies — three of the Nine Sisters of Avalon, it is said — to fetch the king for healing.

Gently they laid King Arthur in the boat, and as Sir Bedivere and Sir Owein watched, the craft moved quietly away from the shore and was lost in the mists that hung over the surface of the lake.

Thus departed the great King Arthur from the world of men into the land of Avalon, where time does not pass, and where all is stillness and quiet save for the song of three magical birds.

Those who hear their song do not die, say the wise folk of Albion, and therefore they believe that one day King Arthur will return; that he will take back the sword from the lake and challenge the darkness of the world with his courage and strength.

The Realm of Albion

The shape of this map follows the outlines of an ancient medieval map of Albion, drawn before cartographers were able to take the exact measurements. The sites of the places named are based on local traditions that speak of the presence of Arthur and his knights, the Ladies of the Lake and other magical beings at these particular locations. However, since Albion is a place of mystery and magic, the castles, cities, forests and lakes where these tales are set can change from day to day, while others may vanish into the mists, never to be seen again.

MAP KEY

1   The Out Isles (Home of King Pellinor)

2   Castle of the Leprous Lady

3   Sarras (City of the Grail)

4   Forest of Inglewood (Here Queen Guinevere saw a Ghost)

5   Joyous Gard (Castle of Sir Lancelot)

6   Merlin's Cave (Here the Wizard hid from his Enemies)

7   The Old Wall (Here Arthur fought the Picts from the North)

8   Castle of Ganis (Home of Sir Bors)

9   The City of Carlisle (King Arthur's Second Great City)

10 Castle of the Fisher King (Home of the Grail Family)

11 The Savage Forest (Home of Sir Ector)

12 Corbenic (Home of Sir Percivale)

13 The Perilous Chapel (Here are Skeleton Knights)

14 Castle of Sir Bercilak

15 The Marvelous Spring (Here Sir Owein became the Guardian)

16 The Green Chapel (Here is the Green Knight)

17 Island of Mon (Here were once Druids)

18 Merlin's Hill (Here the Child Wizard prophesized to King Vortigern)

19 Hautdesert (Home of Sir Bercilak)

20 The Golden Wood (Here begin all Adventures)

21 Bardsey Island (Here Merlin hid the Thirteen Treasures)

22 The Lake (Here live the Nine)

23 Castle of Maidens (Here is a place of Dark Magic)

24 Battle of Camlan (Here King Arthur fought his Last Battle)

25 Dolorous Tower (Here are Dark Knights)

26 Forest of Bedegrayne (Here King Arthur hunted the White Hart)

27 Here King Arthur fought the Battle of the Eleven Kings

28 Tintagel (Here King Arthur was born)

29 Roche Rock (Here Sir Tristan escaped from Prison)

30 Camelot the Golden (Here stands the Round Table)

31 The Sword in the Stone (Here Arthur drew forth the Sword to prove himself King)

32 Castle of Astolat (Home of the Maiden Elaine)

33 St. Michael's Mount (Here Arthur fought a Giant)

34 Castle Dore (Home of King March of Cornouaille)

35 Tristan's Grave (Here the Great Hero lies)

36 Giant's Dance (the Great Circle of Stonehenge)

37 Castle of Keys (Home of Sir Kay)

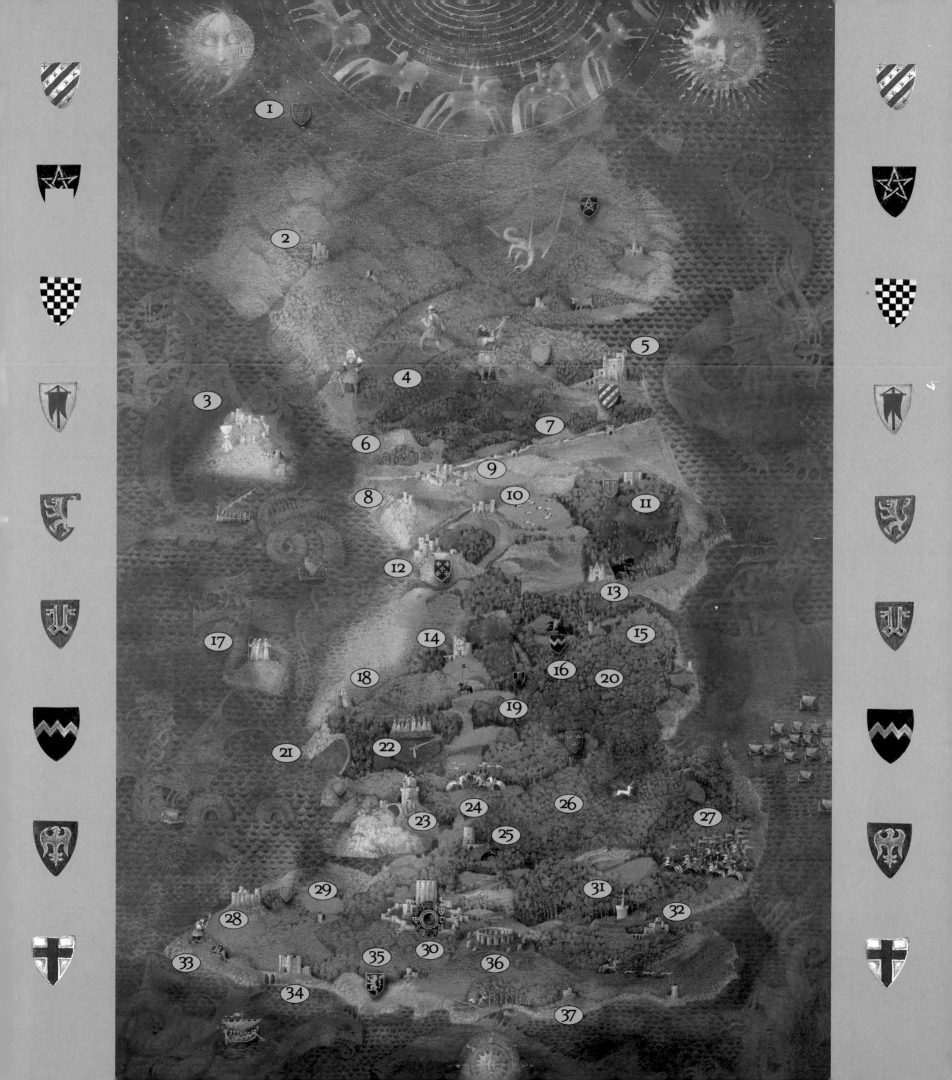

THE AUTHOR

John Matthews has written over a hundred books, many of them about the myths and legends as well as the real history of King Arthur and his knights. He was historical adviser to Jerry Bruckheimer for his film King Arthur of 2004. His book Pirates was number one on the New York Times bestseller list for most of the summer of 2006. John lives in England with his wife, Caitlín, and son, Emrys. His previous projects with Barefoot Books include Giants, Ghosts and Goblins (1999) and Knights (2002). To find out more about John's work and personal appearances, visit his website at www.hallowquest.org.uk.

THE ARTIST

"The world of myths and legends has always inspired writers, composers and artists. For me, it was a great pleasure to illustrate the legends of King Arthur and the Knights of the Round Table." So writes Pavel Tatarnikov, who spent a year in England while working on his breathtaking illustrations for Arthur of Albion.

Pavel was born in 1971 into a family of artists. He has loved drawing since childhood, and his talent was recognized early on: at the age of eleven, he was selected to train at the State School of Music and Fine Arts in Minsk, Belarus. He graduated in 1989 and joined the Graphic Department of the Belarusian Academy of Arts, working as an illustrator. The recipient of many awards, Pavel particularly enjoys projects that combine his love of myths and legends, literature and history. He currently lives in Belarus with his wife, Irina.

Visit his website at www.tatarnikov.com.

FURTHER READING

Kevin Crossley-Holland, the Arthur trilogy:
  The Seeing Stone (Orion, 2001)
  At the Crossing Places (Orion, 2002)
  King of the Middle March (Orion, 2004)
  King Arthur's World (Orion, 2004)

Roger Lancelyn Green:
  King Arthur and His Knights of the Round Table,
  illustrated by Lotte Reiniger
  (Penguin Books, 1953)

Sir Thomas Malory:
  Le Morte d'Arthur, edited by John Matthews,
  illustrated by Anna-Marie Ferguson
  (Orion, 2000)

Caitlín and John Matthews:
  The Arthurian Book of Days: The Greatest Legend
  in the World Retold Throughout the Year
  (Sidgwick & Jackson, 1990)

John Matthews:
  The Song of Arthur (Quest Books, 2000)
  The Song of Taliesin (Quest Books, 2001)
  The Book of Arthur (Vega, 2004)
  King Arthur: Dark Age Warrior and Mythic Hero
  (Carlton Books, 2004)

Christopher Snyder:
  Exploring the World of King Arthur
  (Thames & Hudson, 1999)

Peter Vansittart:
  The Shadow Land (MacDonald, 1967)

Barefoot Books
Celebrating Art and Story

At Barefoot Books, we celebrate art and story that opens

the hearts and minds of children from all walks of life, inspiring

them to read deeper, search further, and explore their own creative gifts.

Taking our inspiration from many different cultures, we focus on themes that

encourage independence of spirit, enthusiasm for learning, and sharing of

the world's diversity. Interactive, playful and beautiful, our products

combine the best of the present with the best of the past to

educate our children as the caretakers of tomorrow.

Live Barefoot!

Join us at www.barefootbooks.com